Dedication

To everyone who has ever felt the tug-of-war between what you know is right and what's easiest to do wrong, this one's for you.

May you learn to recognize the voice of the Liar, roll your eyes at his nonsense, and run straight in to the arms of Truth.

Acknowledgement

My gratitude goes first to the One whom our fictional tempters fear most, for giving wisdom, humor, and the odd ability to write from the wrong perspective without losing my mind.

Thank you to every friend, family member, and fellow believers who has asked hard questions, laughed at the drafts, and reminded me that fiction can still tell the truth.

And finally, to the many unsuspecting humans whose real-life conversations about faith, doubt, and distraction inspired these letters – don't worry, you're safe. Probably.

Dispatches from
the Shadows

Introduction

You are about to eavesdrop on something you were never meant to hear. These pages contain intercepted memos from one tempter to another – internal correspondence from the depths of the Infernal Department of Soul Acquisition. They were never written for human eyes.

Their author, a mid-level operative named Quaver, is neither the brightest nor the most disciplined of his kind. He is, however, devoted to the business of distraction, deception, and slow spiritual erosion. His trainee – whose name you will discover soon enough – is fresh from the lower ranks and still prone to rookie mistakes.

The letters that follow are not theological treatises or neatly packaged devotionals. They are raw instructions, dripping with sarcasm, pride, and the occasional accidental admission that the Enemy (God) is far stronger than Hell's propaganda machine would like to admit.

You'll see the modern temptations discussed in corporate jargon, sins dressed up as self-care, and faith undermined not by grand evil, but by little nudges toward selfishness, laziness, and pride.

Why publish such a thing?

Because, in the right light, the words of a liar make the truth shine all the brighter. By reading Quaver's cynical counsel, you'll begin to notice the same tactics at work in the world around you – and maybe even in your own thinking. And once you see them, they lose much of their power.

So read on, but read with discernment. The author of these memos would be horrified to know you're using them as a survival guide. Which, of course, is exactly why you should.

FROM THE DESK OF:

QUAVER

SENIOR ASSOCIATE TEMPTER
OFFICE 6B, THIRD CIRCLE ANNEX
CENTRAL PIT COMPLEX

My Dear Pipwick,

Congratulations on your recent "promotion" – though I advise you not to let the word go to your head. Around here, a promotion usually means the Department has decided you are just competent enough to be blamed for things but not yet valuable enough to protect from disaster. You will find this arrangement both exhausting and, if you play it right, extremely useful for hiding behind more important demons when things inevitably go wrong.

Before you get sentimental, let me assure you: I did not request you. I had no particular interest in training an apprentice this quarter, much less one fresh from the chaos of the Minor Mischief Division.

I have reviewed your file – impressive that you managed to get yourself nearly dismissed for the butter-on-the-altar incident – and I can see why the Supervisors decided to drop you on my desk.

They think my steady hand can "refine" you into a reliable agent. I think they are hoping you will make me look good before you implode.

Now, to business. You have been assigned your very first human: a moderately religious, moderately ambitious, moderately distracted individual named Elliot Granger. Do not be deceived by the blandness of the profile – the moderately anything are our bread and butter. Passionate sinners often repent when they see the mess they've made, but the mildly selfish, mildly dishonest, mildly disengaged are far easier to keep simmering until their soul is ready for the pot.

You will soon learn the core truth of our work: *our job is not to make them stop believing entirely – our job is to make belief irrelevant to how they live*. Total atheism is a fine outcome, but a distracted, lukewarm believer is often far more valuable to us. They blend in. They rarely cause trouble for our plans. And, most importantly, they can often be persuaded to believe their half-hearted loyalty to the Enemy is, in fact, quite admirable.

Hell is not in the business of producing mass murderers – that's too obvious, too messy.

Our specialty is producing thousands of polite, respectable people who never quite realize they've built their lives facing the wrong direction.

Now, a few rules of engagement before you begin:

Rule One: *Never confront the Enemy directly*. You are not equipped for that. Instead, your job is to keep Elliot busy enough to forget about Him altogether. Do not argue against prayer – make it seem unnecessary today. Do not forbid Scripture – simply suggest that a quick inspirational quote online will suffice. The most dangerous thing for us is a human who has both the time and the clarity to actually listen for the Enemy's voice. Your goal is to ensure Elliot always has a "more urgent" task at hand.

Rule Two: *Exploit the ordinary*. Temptation in the modern age rarely requires horns and fire. It looks like smartphones, endless email threads, small social slights, and Netflix autoplay. We no longer need to fabricate elaborate temptations when humans willingly carry distraction devices in their pockets.

Rule Three: *Bureaucracy is your ally.* I realize you may have thought you joined the grand and glorious army of the Accuser, a fearsome legion against the heavens. In reality, Hell operates much like a poorly managed office. Endless paperwork, misfiled souls, interdepartmental rivalries – all of these serve our purpose quite nicely. The human world mirrors us more than they know, and if we can convince them that meaning is found in climbing ladders, ticking boxes, and keeping up appearances, they will do half our work for us.

Let me also clarify the tone you must take with Elliot's case: subtlety is key. Forget the grand temptations of old. Nobody in the modern era falls for apples on trees. Your weapons will be irritation, self-importance, and mild fatigue. Feed these daily and they will choke spiritual growth before it starts.

Already I can hear you thinking, "But Quaver, wouldn't it be faster to tempt him into outright rebellion?" Oh, my dear incompetent fledgling, rebellion is exhausting to maintain. The Enemy has a most irritating habit of swooping in on rebels with offers of "redemption" and "restoration." But apathy? Now there's a condition that can last decades without raising alarms.

For your first week, I suggest you simply observe him. Take note of the rhythms of his day – when he wakes, how he commutes, what irritates him in traffic, the tone of his conversations with colleagues, his preferred TV shows. Every human has a set of vulnerabilities disguised as harmless preferences. The better you learn his patterns, the more effectively you can disrupt them.

Let me give you an example. If Elliot has a habit of making coffee first thing in the morning, you could ensure that on the day he plans to read his Bible early, the machine malfunctions. Just a tiny inconvenience – but he will tell himself he "can't focus without coffee" and promise to read later. Of course, later never comes.

Finally, a note on our Department culture: You will hear much talk about quotas and performance evaluations. These are not to be taken too seriously. They exist mostly to keep us snapping at each other instead of noticing our collective failures. If you want to survive here, remember this – it's not about actually winning souls (the Upper Management barely tracks individual cases), it's about appearing productive while ensuring no spectacular blunders get noticed by the Enemy's agents.

Now, Pipwick, sharpen your claws and your wits. Keep your report clear, your meddling quiet, and your ego in check. I have little patience for grandstanding, and even less for sentimental musings about "how tragic it is" when they escape our grasp. You will have plenty of time for lamentations when your first assignment collapses in flames – until then, make yourself useful.

Quaver

Yours in persistent subversion,

Quaver

Senior Associate Tempter

Infernal Department of Soul Acquisition

ffice 6B, Third Circle Annex, Central Pit C

INFERNAL DEPARTMENT OF
SOUL ACQUISITION
SUB-DIVISION: MID-TIER HUMAN ACCOUNTS
INTERNAL CORRESPONDENCE— LEVEL Ω

FROM THE DESK OF:

QUAVER

SENIOR ASSOCIATE TEMPTER
OFFICE 6B, THIRD CIRCLE ANNEX
CENTRAL PIT COMPLEX

CONFIDENTIAL — FOR DEMONIC EYES ONLY
UNAUTHOREIZED READING BY HUMANS WILL ESULT
IN IMMEDIATE DISCIPLINARY REVIEW AND/OR THE
REASSIGNMENT OF YOUR MOST PROMISING CASE
TO THE COMPLAINTS DEPARTMENT.

My Dear Pipwick,

You may think our work is about enticing humans into what their kind calls "sin." How quaint. I see they didn't bother to update your training manual past the twelfth century. We've moved on. Modern temptations are less about shoving them off the cliff and more about keeping them perpetually walking in tiny, pointless circles, until they collapse from exhaustion without ever realizing they never left the path.

It is the art of keeping them busy – miserably, perpetually busy – without ever letting them be full. If you do this well, you will never need to tempt them into the "big" moral failures that rookies like you salivate over. Big, flashy sins draw too much attention from the Enemy and His insufferable reinforcements. But the sort of hollow, frantic busyness I'm about to teach? Oh, that's the silent killer. It works slowly, predictably and almost always goes unnoticed.

The beauty of it is that humans practically beg for it. In fact, most of them wear their busyness like a badge of honor. And why wouldn't they? We've spent centuries rebranding "no margin for rest or reflection" into "productivity," "ambition," and my personal favorite – "being a team player."

You have to understand, Pipwick, that the human mind, when slowed down, becomes dangerous to us. Stillness gives them room to hear the Enemy's voice, to think about the meaning of their life, and occasionally to notice the state of their own soul. We can't have that. We need them puffed up with motion and deflated of meaning.

Let's take your human, Elliot. Pleasant fellow, mildly religious, not given to extremes. These are precisely the sort we like to keep running on the treadmill. We don't even have to speed it up. Just make sure he never steps off it.

Your first and most effective tool: **the urgent distraction**. Humans are wired to think that the thing screaming loudest in the moment is the thing that must be done. This is why their devices – marvelous little leashes – are such gifts to us. With a few vibrations and pings, you can ensure Elliot never finishes a thought. Just as he's about to read that devotional?

Oh look, a text from an old friend he hasn't spoken to in months! How thoughtful. He must answer immediately, of course.

And emails – what a treasure. Elliot works in an office, which means email is the bloodstream of his day. A constant drip of "urgent" requests will ensure that even if he plans his morning with noble intentions, by mid-afternoon he'll be telling himself, "I'll pray tonight before bed." You and I both know what "before bed" means: just after scrolling himself into numbness on his phone until his eyelids slam shut.

It is vital you do not try to remove his spiritual habits altogether. That's clumsy. Instead, let him keep them – in shrunken, emaciated form. Five rushed minutes with the Enemy before running out the door feels to a human like "I'm still doing my part." You'll be amazed how quickly they can mistake a nibble for a feast.

Now, onto a subtler move: **social overcommitment**. Humans adore being liked. If you can keep Elliot perpetually saying "yes" – to every committee, every weekend barbecue, every work project – he will confuse approval for purpose. You must whisper that little phrase into his ear: "They need you." Works every time. He'll accept more than he can reasonably handle, because the glow of being wanted is irresistible.

Of course, this requires a delicate touch. You can't let the strain show too soon. If he becomes overtly burned out, he might start pruning commitments – and in pruning, he might accidentally create space for the Enemy. No, keep the pace just shy of collapse. Enough to make him too tired to reflect, but not so tired that others urge him to stop.

Speaking of reflection – teach him to fear it. Stillness, as I've told you, is the soil in which the Enemy's influence grows. So, if Elliot ever has a quiet moment, nudge him toward filling it. Remind him of the podcast he hasn't finished, the news feed he hasn't refreshed, the three unread group chats in his phone. Humans have this delightful, irrational terror of "wasting time." If you keep them convinced that stillness is wasteful, they'll run from it straight into our arms.

And remember, busyness does not require productivity. In fact, the most effective busyness is that which *feels* productive but accomplishes absolutely nothing of eternal worth. You can stuff a day full of errands, social media browsing, and minor household chores, and the human will go to bed convinced they've worked hard. This is one of our finest deceptions – making the meaningless feel meaningful.

You should especially encourage what we call *double distraction*: doing one pointless thing to recover from another pointless thing. He watches television for three hours, feels guilty about it, then "redeems" the evening by reorganizing a drawer full of cables he'll never use. Both activities keep him from prayer. Both are useless. But the combination gives him the sense of balance that will keep him from noticing the truth: he has wasted his day.

Be sure to exploit technology for the slow drip of emptiness. Smartphones are already doing 60% of our work before we lift a claw. Push his notifications just enough to keep his attention splintered. And if he ever thinks of turning them off? Ah, there's where you purr the thought, "But what is someone needs you?" That should keep the leash firmly in place.

Also – and this is important – make him *proud* of his pace. Humans will often boast about their exhaustion as if it's a measure of virtue. Let him equate being "busy" with being "good." If anyone suggests rest, plant the thought that they simply don't understand his important responsibilities. This way, he will defend his own emptiness against those who try to rescue him.

A final thought: give him just enough satisfaction to keep going.

You can't let him realize the deep fatigue in his soul, or he might slow down out of desperation. No, keep feeding him tiny hits of accomplishment – finishing an email chain, clearing his inbox, crossing off a to-do item that didn't matter in the first place. These little victories will make him believe he's in control, even as the real priorities slip away unnoticed.

If you do this well, Pipwick, you'll never have to tempt him into scandal. He'll arrive at the end of his life with a fine resume, a calendar packed with memories of shallow events, and a deep bewilderment at why he feels like something important is missing. By then, of course, it will be too late to fix it.

Now, I expect weekly reports on your progress. Spare me any tales of "Elliot resisted today" unless they come with a plan of how you intend to make him twice as busy tomorrow.
Remember: our best work is not in their falls, but in their drift.

Quaver

Yours in persistent subversion,

Quaver
Senior Associate Tempter
Infernal Department of Soul Acquisition
ffice 6B, Third Circle Annex, Central Pit C

FROM THE DESK OF:

QUAVER

SENIOR ASSOCIATE TEMPTER
OFFICE 6B, THIRD CIRCLE ANNEX
CENTRAL PIT COMPLEX

My Dear Pipwick,

I have reviewed your first report with equal measures of dismay and reluctant amusement. You seem to have grasped the concept of busyness, but you are still fumbling with its execution. You've kept Elliot's schedule pleasantly cluttered, yes, but your distractions lack the sort of persistence that makes them stick like burrs. You still think a distraction is something you throw at a human and hope it works. No, no, my boy – a distraction must be *crafted*, cultivated, and built into the very air they breathe until it becomes their default state. They must not simply be distracted; they must become the sort of creature for whom focus is unnatural.

Allow me to instruct you in the proper art of distraction.

Your objective is not merely to keep his eyes off the Enemy, but to make it so that when the Enemy stands directly before him, Elliot's mind is already so clouded with noise that he does not notice. We are not just talking about the obvious baubles – the glowing screens, the trivial hobbies, the half-finished projects. We are talking about a whole environment of distraction in which the human swims like a fish in murky water, unable to imagine that clarity was ever possible.

The first principle is variety. A single distraction, however tempting, will eventually grow stale. Yes, Elliot might become obsessed with his phone for a week, checking it every few minutes. But leave him to that alone and he will tire of it; worse, the Enemy might whisper to him in a moment of boredom and lure him back to attention. You must rotate distractions with the skill of a juggler. Move him from his television to his work tasks, from his work tasks to some trivial household project. Keep the wheels spinning so quickly that he forgets he is on a ride at all.

The second principle is layering. The clever tempter never uses distractions in isolation.

One must bleed into another so seamlessly that the human never registers the shift. Picture this: Elliot sits down to watch "just one episode" of a harmless show. During the credits, his phone pings. While responding to a message, he notices an advertisement for some product. He clicks the link, which leads to a news article, which links to another article, which suggests a related video. Before he knows it, two hours have passed, his tea is cold, and the Bible reading he meant to do has been quietly buried under the digital avalanche. And the best part? He will believe it all "just happened," never suspecting your hand at the tiller.

Now, as for the tools at your disposal, modern humanity has furnished us with more than we could have dreamed in centuries past. We used to have to work through physical diversions – parties, gossip, card games, long pointless errands. Now they carry distraction devices in their pockets, and most of them sleep with the thing's inches form their faces. Exploit this with relentless precision. A human attention span is a fragile thing, and with the right nudges, you can keep it fractured into so many tiny shards that it cannot reflect a single coherent thought.

Social media is one of our finest weapons. Do not underestimate its capacity for endless loops of envy, outrage, and shallow amusement.

The trick is to keep Elliot checking it even when nothing particularly interesting is happening. If you can train him to reach for his phone in every idle moment – waiting for the kettle to boil, standing in line, even walking to the car – you will have stolen from him every one of the small silences in which the Enemy could have whispered.

News cycles are equally delicious. Humans are capable of convincing themselves that they "must stay informed" when in fact what they crave is the little thrill of anger or anxiety each headline brings. Keep Elliot checking news feeds multiple times a day. Better yet, encourage him to follow several contradictory sources so that he is perpetually unsettled, never sure what's true but always sure that Something Must Be Done. In this way, you can fill his mind with a constant undercurrent of irritation and helplessness – fertile soil for the seeds of despair.

Another effective tactic is the cultivation of trivial curiosities. Humans have an admirable capacity to obsess over things that do not matter in the slightest.

Encourage Elliot to fall down rabbit holes –
learning obscure facts about celebrities he will
never meet, becoming deeply invested in the
statistics of a sports team's performance, or
memorizing the specifications of some gadget
he will never buy. You might think such pursuits
are harmless, but remember: every hour spent
on them is an hour not spent strengthening his
spiritual muscles.

One of my personal favorites is the art of turning
good things into distractions. The Enemy has, for
some reason, stocked their world with pleasant
and wholesome pursuits – music, art, gardening,
friendship. Left in His hands, these things can
refresh a human's soul. But with a little work,
you can transform them into idols of distraction.
Let Elliot start a new hobby – not because it
brings him joy or connection, but because it
gives him something else to prioritize over
prayer. Nudge him to spend more on equipment
than on effort, to fuss over details instead of
savoring the experience. Soon he will be
consumed not by the beauty of the hobby but by
the logistics of maintaining it, which is far safer
for us.

It is also wise to interrupt important moments
with entirely unimportant ones.

If Elliot ever begins to think deeply during a sermon or a conversation, whisper the reminder that he forgot to set the oven timer. If he is praying and beginning to feel genuinely present, nudge him with the urge to jot down a to-do item before he forgets. You must teach him to value the security of his lists over the uncertainty of reflection.

Above all, remember that distraction must become his refuge. Life will throw Elliot moments of discomfort – boredom, grief, frustration. In these moments, the Enemy might, if given the chance, break through with comfort or guidance. Your job is to make sure Elliot never faces such discomfort without reaching for distraction. Let him believe that silence is unbearable, that stillness is a waste, that his mind is something to be constantly entertained rather than examined. If you can make distraction his automatic response to pain or unease, you will have forged a chain he will never think to break.

And here's the subtle twist you must learn to master: guilt is not always the enemy of distraction – sometimes it is its best friend. If Elliot spends an evening watching videos instead of helping his wife with some task, and he feels guilty, you might think that's a crack the Enemy could use. But you can twist it.

Make him so uncomfortable with the guilt that he reaches for another distraction to smother it. In this way, the guilt itself becomes one more reason to avoid reflection.

Do not neglect physical distractions either. A cluttered, noisy environment is ideal. Suggest to Elliot that he always keep the television or music on in the background, even when he's not paying attention to it. Let him believe he "works better with noise." The constant hum will keep his mind from wandering anywhere useful. Encourage him to leave tasks half-done so that there's always a small nagging sense of incompletion – a perfect seed for further distraction.

As you weave these threads together, be patient. Distraction works best when it becomes invisible. Elliot must never feel as though he is being pulled from something important. He must believe he is simply following his interests, responding to life as it comes. Over time, his mind will lose the capacity for depth, and the Enemy's voice will become like a faint signal on a broken radio. He will not reject the voice outright; he will simply no longer have the patience to listen.

This is the true genius of our craft, Pipwick. We do not need to chain them to the floor. We need only scatter enough glitter on the ground that they never look up.

I expect better results in your next report. Do not tell me you "tried" a distraction. Distraction is not an event – it is a climate. You are not tossing pebbles into his path; you are building him a home in the fog.

Quaver

Yours in persistent subversion,

Quaver
Senior Associate Tempter
Infernal Department of Soul Acquisition
ffice 6B, Third Circle Annex, Central Pit C

**INFERNAL DEPARTMENT OF
SOUL ACQUISITION**

SUB-DIVISION: MID-TIER HUMAN ACCOUNTS
INTERNAL CORRESPONDENCE— LEVEL Ω

FROM THE DESK OF:

QUAVER

SENIOR ASSOCIATE TEMPTER
OFFICE 6B, THIRD CIRCLE ANNEX
CENTRAL PIT COMPLEX

CONFIDENTIAL — FOR DEMONIC EYES ONLY
UNAUTHOREIZED READING BY HUMANS WILL ESULT
IN IMMEDIATE DISCIPLINARY REVIEW AND/OR THE
REASSIGNMENT OF YOUR MOST PROMISING CASE
TO THE COMPLAINTS DEPARTMENT.

My Dear Pipwick,

It has come to my attention – via that appalling smug report you submitted – that you are still treating Elliot's "faith" as something to be dismantled outright. How tiresome. Did I not tell you that direct assault is the surest way to lose him? Strike at it too openly and you will provoke him to defend it. You might as well wave a red flag at a sleeping bull. Our craft is subtler, slower, and infinitely more satisfying when done properly.

If you must meddle with his religion, the key is not to oppose it but to dilute it. The human spiritual life is rather like tea – a little strong when steeped properly, but easily turned into lukewarm flavored water if you keep topping up the cup without ever replacing the leaves. Yes, let him keep reading the Enemy's Book. Let him keep attending that weekly gathering of His tiresome followers. Let him even pray.

But see to it that all of these are done in such a way that nothing of substance is absorbed.

The best starting point is his expectations. Humans approach their faith practices with certain unspoken hopes: comfort, insight, a sense of connection. The more these expectations are disappointed, the less eager they are to continue. This is where you must get creative. If Elliot begins to pray, nudge his thoughts toward the clock. If he opens the Book, let his eyes glide over the words while his mind chews on the meeting he has after lunch. When he goes to his gathering, make sure the person sitting next to him fidgets just enough to annoy. In short – fill the practice with small irritations until the practice itself feels irritating.

You must also exploit the humans' tragic hunger for novelty. Once the shine of something wears off, they assume it is no longer "working." If Elliot has been reading the same passage for several days, whisper that perhaps he should find something "more relevant" or "fresh." Keep him flitting from one section to another, never settling long enough to absorb anything. This works especially well with devotional books – they are full of bite-sized readings, easy to consume and easier to forget.

There is another deliciously subtle approach: encourage the performance of faith without the participation of the heart. This is one of our department's oldest tricks, and for good reason. If Elliot can be persuaded that the Enemy is impressed by mere attendance and outward politeness, you will have converted his faith into a sort of weekly costume party. Have him sit in the service thinking about how good it is that he came, regardless of whether he listened to a word. Let him pray in words so rehearsed that his own mind dozes off halfway through. And if the Enemy actually tries to nudge him into a moment of real engagement – perhaps through a verse or a song – well, that's the moment you cough gently in his thoughts and remind him of the grocery list.

Speaking of which, the grocery list is an underappreciated spiritual weapon. In moments of prayer or meditation, suggest to him just one urgent item – milk, toothpaste, the bill that needs paying. He will naturally tell himself he'll "just write it down" so he won't forget. You and I both know that within moments, his mind will have wandered from milk to dinner plans, to an argument he once had with a colleague three years ago, and by the time he remembers he was praying, the moment will be gone.

Do not neglect the role of fatigue. If Elliot is tired enough, even the Enemy's clearest words will slide off his mind like rain on oiled cloth. Encourage late nights for trivial reasons. If he thinks of going to bed on time, whisper that he's "earned a little relaxation" and that one more episode, one more round of scrolling, one more chapter in the novel won't hurt. The next morning, when his faith practices feel dull and lifeless, he will assume the fault lies in the practices themselves – never realizing it is his own exhaustion that has numbed him.

It is also worth turning his attention to the faults of others. Nothing spoils the spiritual palate like the taste of self-righteousness. If, during a church service, you can get him thinking about how off-key the singing is, or how poorly dressed the man in front of him appears, or how the preacher's tone reminds him of someone he dislikes, you will have shifted his focus entirely away from the Enemy. Soon, the gatherings will become exercises in criticism rather than worship.

One of the more refined strategies is to let him feel a mild pride in his faithfulness. The moment he congratulates himself for being a "regular" at church or for "reading every day," you can begin to feed the idea that he has already reached an acceptable plateau in his spiritual life.

From there, it is a small step to complacency. Complacency is, in many ways, the crown jewel of our work. A complacent believer is like a soldier who insists on keeping his armor polished but never wears it into battle.

You should also keep a close eye on any attempts he makes to discuss spiritual matters with others. Humans can be dangerously encouraged by such conversations if they are genuine. So, if Elliot tries to share his thoughts, make sure the conversation gets tangled in trivial disagreements or is quickly derailed into talking about the weather, the news, or some recent television program. The key is not to silence him, but to ensure that nothing of substance is exchanged.

If the Enemy's voice becomes too persistent in his practices, you may have to employ the "to-do list swap." This is where you let Elliot feel as though he is doing something spiritual while actually doing something entirely different. He might think he is praying for a friend's need, but you gently slide his thoughts toward planning how he will phrase his own news when they next speak. He might open the Bible intending to read, but end up looking for a verse to support an opinion he already holds. This way, the motions continue but the meaning is gone.

And here is where you must be patient. The erosion of faith practices is like the wearing away of stone by water. Do not expect a single day's work to make them crumble. Instead, let the small silt of distraction and disinterest build up until the stream no longer flows. The most beautiful part? Elliot will tell himself he "still believes" all the right things, and because the words are still in his head, he will assume the reality is still in his heart.

The truth, Pipwick – which you must never admit to anyone, least of all yourself – is that the Enemy is perfectly capable of reviving the faintest spark into a flame if the human is truly willing. That is why our work must be to keep them *unwilling* without ever saying so outright. Let Elliot believe he is already fine, that nothing needs changing, and that the dullness he feels is simply "the way things are."

When you can watch him sit through a service unmoved, read a chapter without remembering a word, and pray without noticing the silence in his own heart, then, my boy, you will have graduated from apprentice to professional.

Quaver

Yours in persistent subversion,

Quaver
Senior Associate Tempter
Infernal Department of Soul Acquisition
ffice 6B, Third Circle Annex, Central Pit C

FROM THE DESK OF:

QUAVER

SENIOR ASSOCIATE TEMPTER
OFFICE 6B, THIRD CIRCLE ANNEX
CENTRAL PIT COMPLEX

CONFIDENTIAL — FOR DEMONIC EYES ONLY
UNAUTHOREIZED READING BY HUMANS WILL ESULT
IN IMMEDIATE DISCIPLINARY REVIEW AND/OR THE
REASSIGNMENT OF YOUR MOST PROMISING CASE
TO THE COMPLAINTS DEPARTMENT.

Dear Pipwick,
I have read your latest account on Elliot's habits
and, while I am pleased to see you've learned to
keep him spinning like a plate on a wobbling
stick, I worry you still do not grasp the appetites
that drive him. Busyness is a splendid leash, yes,
but leashes snap when a beast sees meat. You
must learn to bait him with pleasures – familiar,
respectable, perfectly defensible pleasures –
and let those do the pulling. Any fool can throw a
snare. A professional builds a garden path lined
with sweets.

Humans like to imagine that pleasure belongs to
the Enemy, as if He cornered the market and we
deal only in gray gruel and ashes. Hilarious,
really. The Enemy may have made the raw
materials, but we discovered a secret.

He never admits in polite company: almost any
pleasure, detached from its proper place and
time and proportion, turns into a quiet engine for

undoing the very creature who enjoys it. Nothing so effectively ruins a soul as a good thing treated as a god.

Being where Elliot is already compliant. He is not, as you have noted, decadent. No scarlet lamps. No obvious vices. He is pleasant, moderate, and (this is our opening) quietly tired. Tired people do not need new temptations; they need excuses to overuse the ones they already have. Look at the table of his day and ask: where does he reward himself? That reward – however innocent – must be cultivated into refuge. Refuge must become ritual. And the ritual, at last, must become the master.

Start small. The evening "treat." You have reported, he likes to unwind with a show and a snack after the day. Very good. Remove the shame from it and replace it with entitlement. Murmur, "You've earned it." Not the brash entitlement of the glutton; the mild, cardigan-wrapped entitlement of the respectable worker who would never call it gluttony, only comfort. He will add a second episode. Then a third. He will upgrade the snack. None of this will look like a fall – merely a cozy slope.
On the slope, you are always moving and always able to say you haven't moved very far.

The aim is never the quantity alone, you simpleton. The aim is dependency. The line to cross is the one where human says, "I cannot relax without this." Notice the pronoun. Not "I cannot relax," which might trigger alarm, but "without this," which sounds precise, practical, almost healthful. When the doormat reads "*This House Runs on Chocolate and Streaming*," you have arrived.

Do not imagine pleasure only happens in the mouth or on the sofa. Elliot's job can be pleasure, too – not in the Enemy's sense of vocation but in the quiet narcotic of feeling effective. He likes being competent. Excellent. Help him worship the sensation. When he is praised, fan it. When he finishes a task, let a warm light pool in his chest and whisper, "More of this, now." If his colleagues appreciate him, make their faces into candles he must keep lit. Soon, he will chase the glow all day, and any activity that does not offer immediate warmth – prayer, patience, listening – will seem cold and therefore wrong.

A side note on food and drink: avoid the obvious conduits unless Elliot is already leaning that way. If you make him a lush, you'll wake patrols. Instead, favor *precision gourmetship*. Teach him to become exacting. Not a drunk – perish the thought – an enthusiast.

He will read about beans, grinds, regions, notes of caramel and whispers of citrus in his morning coffee. He will learn to pour at precisely ninety-three degrees. He will time the bloom. This is not about the tongue. It is about the clock. He will spend the time he once gave the Enemy to his kettle's hiss and call it artistry. And you will clap, quiet as ash.

Pleasure works best where it can impersonate gratitude. If he says grace over his plate, let him couple the prayer with the menu. "Thank you for this abundance," and then, unspoken, "and for the right to arrange daily life around it." You must never attack thanksgiving – that will shock him. You must fuse thanksgiving to preference so tightly he cannot tell them apart. Consequently, any hindrance to preference will feel like an assault on gratitude itself. If his child interrupts the ritual of evening relaxation, he will not say, "My preference was thwarted." He will say, "I am not allowed any peace." Victimhood is pleasure's final spice.

You are too crude with bodily appetite. A nudge here: the eye is more pliable than the flesh. Do not hustle him toward scandal. Train his gaze to seek minor delights that graze the borderlands of impropriety and then feign innocence.

An advertisement that lingers a fraction too long, a "suggested post" with soft edges – never obscene, merely suggestive, like a door left ajar. The mind will take the tour on its own, and when conscience clears its throat, our choicest response is a shrug: *It was nothing.* If you repeat "nothing" often enough, the category of "something" shrinks, until he can comfortably deny the very act of looking as attention at all.

Recreation is a luscious orchard. You wrote that Elliot jogs when the weather is kind. Marvelous. Help him turn the loop around the block into liturgy. Preach to him about heart rates and personal bests and equipment. Buy him a watch – better, let him buy three, comparing metrics across brands. He must never run without the thought of being watched, graphed, measured. Let him check the chart after prayer and, slowly, instead of prayer. He will tell himself that caring for the body is godly stewardship. Quite. And the soul? Hush, later. The graph is spiking. Praise be.

Ah, marital affection – do mind your boots here. We are forbidden the old wrecking-ball approach unless invited; even then, it tends to rouse defenders. The delicate method is to introduce scorekeeping into affection. Keep it all tender, of course; we do not want fights, we want ledgers. He gives a kindness; he expects a kindness returned in the same wrapping.

He listens; he wants to be listened to – in his manner and on his schedule. Affection as currency is still affection. Only transactional. The pleasure remains, but the taste grows needful and exact. When the exchange fails, he feels cheated. Cheated men grow peevish. Peevish men pray less.

Music can be a sacrament to either kingdom. Let him assemble playlists for every moment – focus, chores, sleep, shower, commute – until silence feels like a mistake. He must never allow quiet to persist long enough to discover the Enemy's unnerving knack for turning quiet into Presence. And keep the volume just beneath complaint. He must not notice it, only need it.

The Sabbath – such a maddening invention. The Enemy intends it for rest, delight, holy attentiveness. We can invert all three. Rest becomes lethargy; delight becomes indulgence; attentiveness becomes binging. Give him a "Sabbath treat" – a pastry, a football marathon, an hours-long soak in feeds – so he will spend the day managing his treats instead of receiving the day as gift. By evening he will feel heavy and weirdly hollow. Perfect. He will assume the day itself did this to him. Then he will quietly avoid it next week, replacing the "useless rest day" with necessary chores. Harsh yoke resumed, he will claim relief.

I told you once that the finest bait is a good thing at the wrong time. Now hear its twin: the right thing in the wrong measure. Encourage enthusiasm to go just a half-turn too far – hobbies into identities, preferences into banners, tastes into tribes. The pleasure of belonging is a hot little coal. If he warms himself there, he will begin to view those outside his taste-tribe with faint suspicion. Suspicion is the great un-prayer, a steady murmur that drowns gratitude like a faucet left running.

And please stop assuming pleasure must be tactile. Intellectual pleasure might be the most potent of all, because it returns to its trough without shame. Feed Elliot's enjoyment of being "in the know." Let him become the fellow with the interesting fact. Notice: not the true fact, the interesting one. There is a difference, and the difference is where we live. His friends will reward him with that little widening of the eyes. The widening is a drug. Soon he will require it. He will shop his thoughts at conversations like a vendor, checking which sell. Prayer will feel like a market with no customers, and he will close early.

You asked, idiot boy, whether we should allow him the simple pleasures the Enemy approves – walks, laughter, shared meals. Allow? We must curate them.

Laughter is safest when unshared, directed at a screen, carefully timed to ensure no lingering in the warm afterglow of a friend's presence. Walks are best when tracked. Shared meals are harmless if photographed before the first bite. Remember, anything experienced is a thread the Enemy may pull. Anything displayed is a thread we hold.

Let us speak of threshold, because you will not notice them unless I paint them in fire. The first threshold in the pleasure trap is *permission*: from "I may" to "I should." The second is *pattern*: from "I sometimes" to "I always." The third is protection: from "I enjoy" to "I must not be deprived." After protection comes *protest*: the stage at which any interference, however gentle, becomes an injustice. A man defending his treat is a soldier in our army and does not know it.

You can accelerate these stages with scarcity. Make his day feel narrow – too many duties, too little kindness. Then his evening feels like a ration line, and rations awaken the hoarder. He will stack pleasures for later with a dragon's eye. Woe to the spouse or child who disturbs the arrangements. Woe – then sulk – then distance. The Enemy calls the table "fellowship." We call it "interruptible."

Ah, and the body. The Enemy carved pleasure into its very seams. We cannot evict pleasure; we can only redirect habit. A tired body reaches for sugar, salt, and softness. Give them in the late hour. The next morning the body is full, and dull bodies reach for shortcuts, and shortcuts are where prayer goes to be postponed. We do not need him wicked. We need him unready. Translate every appetite into lateness, lethargy, and then into the claim that the Enemy's way is too strenuous for modern schedules.

Do not be fooled by Elliot's occasional pangs of conscience. They are not the cavalry; they are – if we are quick – seasoning. Shame makes man hide. We dangle comfort like a curtain. He ducks behind it for "just a minute" and emerges at midnight, blinking at the clock as if it pulled him. Your job is to keep the curtain within reach. Easy curtains: the arm of a sofa, the soft light of a kitchen at eleven, the glowing orchard of a phone. Hard curtains: a book with pages that do not refresh. Discourage the hard ones. Encourage the easy.

You worry he may notice the emptiness. He will. Let him. Then supply a plausible explanation. "You need a better series." "You need a higher-end grinder." "You need a weekend away where you can finally indulge properly."

The indulgence must always be the remedy for the previous indulgence's failure. Thus, we transform disappointment into a sales channel.

If he stumbles on the Enemy's old warning about idols, reinterpret them as rustic poetry. "Surely," he will say, "they did not mean this." Let him draw a circle around ancient statues and keep his modern altars anonymous: Subscription, Preference, Brand, Routine. Have him donate those altars a tithe of attention each day. He will call it self-care. He will not notice he is being cared for by objects.

The safest arena to anchor all this is the bugger between pain and prayer. When he hurts, if he reaches first for pleasure (even the innocent sort), we win the hinge of his life. You need not forbid prayer; simply let it come second. Second prayers dry on the tongue. He will get there, yes, after the snack, after the scroll, after the bath – by which time his soul is lulled. He will offer the Enemy a yawn and call it devotion. Each night he signs the treaty anew.

As to church – stop trembling – pleasure loves pews. Teach him to prefer a particular style of song, a preferred tempo, a precise homiletical flavor. If the service deviates, he suffers and concludes he "didn't get much out of it." Notice the pronoun again.

Church becomes a dispenser. When it dispenses what he likes, he approves the machinery. When it does not, he withholds desire. This posture is not hostile; it is just...seated. But pews are furnaces when seated wrong.

Now listen carefully, because this is where apprentices trip over their own tails. We do not wish to make him a caricature. An obvious glutton, a brazen hedonist, a cackling collector of limited editions – such men are either rescued by dramatic inventions or avoided by everyone useful to us. Elliot must remain the sort who could nod at a proverb about self-control and sincerely agree while polishing a shrine made of small habits. The shrine must look like a shelf.

Do not underestimate how quickly good, clean pleasures will defend themselves with scripture fragments. He will recite "every creature is good" while taking a third portion he does not want. He will quote "the earth is the Lord's" while rearranging his week around a tasting menu. He will invoke "Sabbath made for man" while building a day that starts with sloth, crescendos in frenzy, and ends in numbness. If you are patient, he will do your arguing for you with a concordance in his lap.
Shall we speak of children? Danger – but not if you nudge, not shove.

Children dilute and intensify pleasure. They wreck the neat rituals, then replace them with louder ones. Encourage the father to resent the wreckage and secretly envy the intensity. Let him call his envy "concern" and his resentment "boundaries." He will demand pockets of untouched pleasure as compensation for fatherhood's weather. His spouse will oblige reluctantly. Resentment will learn to count.

Finally, reinforce the one confession that completes the cage: I deserve this. Not shouted. Breathed. He will never say it in prayer; he will say it to the refrigerator light. He will say it by tapping the "Are you still watching?" prompt. He will say it by standing a moment longer in the hot water. He will not shout because he is not proud of it. He will whisper because whispers are prayers for us.

You have until next week to show me proof of dependency. I want to read that he tried to pray and decided to treat himself first. I want to read that he postponed an act of ordinary service because the timing was awkward for his ritual. I want to read that he explained himself to his conscience in paragraphs. Then, my little gourmand of secondhand sins, I will know you have learned to set a table.

Quaver

Yours in persistent subversion,

Quaver
Senior Associate Tempter
Infernal Department of Soul Acquisition
ffice 6B, Third Circle Annex, Central Pit C

FROM THE DESK OF:

QUAVER

SENIOR ASSOCIATE TEMPTER
OFFICE 6B, THIRD CIRCLE ANNEX
CENTRAL PIT COMPLEX

My Dear Pipwick,

I see from your latest report that you are still keeping Elliot well-stocked with busyness and distractions. Admirable, in a novice sort of way. But you seem to have neglected one of our most effective strategies: training him to measure his worth in the eyes of the others rather than in the eyes of the Enemy. If you can manage this, you will hardly need to tempt him in any other way; he will live and die by the praise and approval of those around him, chasing it like a thirsty man chasing the shadow of a well.

Understand this: humans are hardwired to notice themselves in the reflection of others. They peer into the eyes of friends, colleagues, strangers on a bus, and search for confirmation of who they are. The Enemy intends this for mutual encouragement, that they might spur each other on to virtue.

We, however, can twist it into a treadmill of performance – one that never stops, never satisfies, and wears the soul to threadbare.

Begin subtly. The direct "you must be liked at all costs" approach is far too obvious; some of them will spot the snare. Instead, plant the thought that "it's good to be respected" – which is true enough to pass without suspicion – and then slowly, imperceptibly, replace the word respected with admired. The shift is almost invisible. Respected people can sometimes be unpopular; admired people are careful never to be. And to be admired, one must adjust constantly, shaping oneself to the mood and taste of the room. This is the heart of the trap.

One of the most elegant methods is to nudge him toward counting. Counting what? Anything that can be tallied and compared. Social media followers, compliments received, "likes" on his pictures, the number of people who greet him at church, how many colleagues invite him to lunch. Counting creates the illusion of measurable worth, but the numbers are never high enough. The moment he surpasses one figure, the next becomes the goal. Keep him in this loop and he will never have the stillness to ask whether the Enemy's opinion might be the only one that matters.

You can also use harmless-seeming conversations to reinforce this hunger. When someone praises him, amplify the warmth he feels. Let it linger. Let him replay it later in the shower or as he drives to work. Encourage him to relive the tone, the look, the approving nod. The more he savors it, the more he will seek it. And the more he seeks it, the more he will compromise in tiny, almost invisible ways to get it.

Another fertile soil for approval-seeking is service. The Enemy prizes service done quietly, for its own sake. We must prize service that is noticed and remarked upon. Encourage Elliot to volunteer for things that put him in front of others, or to make sure his contributions are mentioned aloud. If he must serve in unseen ways, suggest small ways to "share" about it afterwards – purely, of course, so others can be "encouraged." The human tongue is marvelously good at wrapping pride in humility's clothing.

And then there's comparison. Oh, Pipwick, never underestimate comparison! It is the breeding ground of both pride and insecurity, those twin poisons that can live comfortably in the same heart. Let him measure his house against the neighbor's, his children's achievements against those of his friends, his career progress against people from his graduating class.

Make sure that whether he is ahead or behind, he feels it deeply. If he's ahead, you can feed him smugness; if he's behind, feed him envy. Both turn his eyes away from the Enemy's standard and toward the endlessly shifting standard of everyone else.

Church life, as usual, provides its own delightful opportunities. Encourage him to compare himself to "those people" who don't seem as committed, as generous, as wise. Let him measure sermons by how well they align with his own opinions, and conversations by how much he feels valued in them. The goal is to make worship gatherings less about encountering the Enemy and more about securing a certain social standing. A man can sit in the same pew for years under this enchantment without ever realizing he's praying to the crowd instead of the creator.

And be sure to use silence against him. If someone doesn't respond to a text, make him wonder what they think of him. If he greets a friend and they seem distracted, whisper that perhaps they are upset with him. Such moments, repeated often enough, can keep him in a low-grade anxiety that demands constant reassurance from others. That reassurance, when it comes, will soothe him briefly before the hunger returns. In this way, you can make him a slave to the next nod, the next smile, the next "good job."

Now, you must also learn to weaponize failure. If Elliot falls short of someone's expectations – real or imagined – use the moment to either drive him into despair or make him double his efforts to please. In despair, he will avoid situations where the Enemy might use him, convinced he is unworthy. In overcompensation, he will exhaust himself doing things the Enemy never asked of him, leaving little energy for the things He did. Both outcomes are equally acceptable to us.

One more thing: be sure to keep his sense of self tied to roles rather than to reality. Let him think of himself as "the helpful one," and then make him panic whenever something threatens that label. If someone else is praised for a skill he prides himself on, make it sting. If he fails in the role, make it feel catastrophic. Roles are brittle things; when they crack, the human inside them is often too stunned to remember who he is beyond them.

Do not rush this work, Pipwick. Approval addiction is not built overnight. It is grown, layer by layer, like a pearl in reverse – with grit on the outside and a hollow center.

In time, Elliot will become so accustomed to chasing the next approving glance that the Enemy's gaze will feel distant, abstract, and far less urgent. That is when you can leave him to run on autopilot, confident that every choice he makes will be filtered through the question, "What will they think of me?"

When that day comes, he will no longer need you to keep him from the Enemy's will. He will keep himself from it, not out of rebellion, but out of the mistaken belief that other people's smiles are the truest sign of righteousness. And when you've trained a man to confuse applause with holiness, you can sit back and call the case nearly closed.

I expect progress in this line by the next report. Do not bring me another tedious list of small talk and social events; bring me signs that he is adjusting himself like a mirror to every face he meets, unable to stand unless someone else tells him how tall he is.

Quaver

Yours in persistent subversion,

Quaver
Senior Associate Tempter
Infernal Department of Soul Acquisition
ffice 6B, Third Circle Annex, Central Pit C

INFERNAL DEPARTMENT OF
SOUL ACQUISITION

SUB-DIVISION: MID-TIER HUMAN ACCOUNTS
INTERNAL CORRESPONDENCE— LEVEL Ω

FROM THE DESK OF:

QUAVER

SENIOR ASSOCIATE TEMPTER
OFFICE 6B, THIRD CIRCLE ANNEX
CENTRAL PIT COMPLEX

My Dear Pipwick,

It has dawned on me – slowly, like the unpleasant awareness of a damp sock – that you still haven't learned the difference between a temptation and a trajectory. Temptations are momentary; trajectories are lifestyles. You've been handing Elliot temptations like someone feeding peanuts to a distracted elephant. Yes, he eats them. But he's still going wherever he was going before. What I'm teaching you is how to rewire the compass entirely so that he drifts in our direction without ever realizing he's left the trail.

Today's lesson: the corrosion of truth – not by outright lies,
(you're not clever enough to keep those airtight),
but by gentle distortion. If you can distort Elliot's understanding of truth, he will no longer recognize the Enemy's voice when he hears it. And when a man can't tell the difference between his Shepherd and a sales pitch, well...we can sell him anything.

The first and most obvious avenue is the person filter. Every human hears what he wants to hear and discards the rest – the Enemy calls them to listen with open hearts, but our business is to train them to listen with loaded expectations. Before Elliot even cracks open that wretched Book, whisper to him what he's hoping to find. Make him seek confirmation of his opinions rather than correction of them. That way, even when he's "reading," he's only hunting for words to weaponize in his own arguments.

I recall a rather satisfying case handled by Jarks over in the Department of Doctrinal Fog. His man started with a harmless disagreement about the best way to interpret a single verse. Within five years, the fellow could not attend a single Bible study without derailing it into his pet topic. Eventually, he stopped attending altogether because "no one else took Scripture seriously." What Jarks had actually done was teach the man to treat truth like a coat tailor-made for himself – cut to his measurements, hemmed to his tastes, altered whenever it felt tight. Elliot must be taught to do the same.

The modern world, thankfully, makes this easier than ever. Humans have surrounded themselves with echo chambers – little padded rooms of opinion where they only ever hear voices that agree with them. Technology, for once, has been an absolute gift to us. Keep Elliot's feeds filled with sources that parrot what he already believes. When the Enemy tries to slip in a perspective that might challenge him, the cognitive static will be so loud he won't even notice it.

But do not stop at the information level. We want him to feel truth, not test it. This is essential. If something feels right to him – comforting, affirming, flattering – let him label it as "my truth." The Enemy's idea of truth is fixed and external, like the sun – always there, regardless of how one feels about it. We prefer the idea of truth as a lava lamp – warm, shifting, endlessly customizable.

Now, be careful not to make him a raving relativist too soon. That stench can be detected by even the sleepiest conscience. Instead, ease him into the notion that "what's true for me may not be true to others," but only in areas where he doesn't want accountability.
You'll find this especially useful when dealing with moral instructions that inconvenience him. The Enemy says, "Do this,' and we nudge, "Well, maybe you don't feel called to do that."

Another efficient method is to sow suspicion of authority – but only selective suspicion.

Don't make him distrust all leaders; just the ones who might actually guide him toward the Enemy. This way, he'll reject sermons, books, and conversations that could help him, while swallowing whole the opinions of celebrities, influencers, and charming but shallow acquaintances. Humans are excelled at thinking they're "thinking for themselves" while being puppeted by whoever flatters them most.

Let's talk about memory, Pipwick, because memory is the rust that eats the hull of truth. Get him to remember selectively. When he recalls a time the Enemy helped him, blur the details until it feels like coincidence. When he remembers a time, he was corrected, frame it as an attack on his character. The more you can distort his memory of events, the less reliable his grasp on truth will be. A man whose memories are all edited will trust nothing but his current feelings – and feelings are the most cooperative of servants if you know how to feed them.

This reminds me of a delicious fiasco courtesy of Ravel, one of the laziest tempters I've ever met. His man once endured a real trial – the sort the Enemy uses to forge stubbornly resilient faith. But Ravel got him to believe that the entire season was pointless, that nothing good came of it, and that the Enemy had been cruel to allow it.

The man now avoids prayer entirely, citing "past disappointments." Ravel didn't need to invent a lie – he just let the man's memory calcify in resentment. Keep that trick handy.

Of course, the ultimate goal is distorting truth, not to make Elliot deny it outright (that's amateur stuff) but to make him uninterested in it. That's when the rot sets in. If he believes truth is unknowable, or too complicated to bother with, he'll content himself with whatever feels right in the moment. At that point, the Enemy's words will sound like a foreign language he once studied in school but forgot after the exam.

Now, I must warn you: some tempters try to skip straight to cynicism – the belief that everyone lies, so why bother believing anything? That's sloppy work. Cynicism can backfire; it can drive humans to search desperately for something certain, which the Enemy is only too happy to provide. No, we want Elliot to believe that truth exists but that he already has enough of it. That way, he'll never go looking for more.
As you work, keep the corrosion invisible. When steel rusts slowly, the ship sails on, unaware of the holes forming below the waterline. One day, it sinks – and everyone pretends to be shocked.

Oh, and do keep yourself entertained. In the Department of Subtle Revision, we often run contests to see who can plant the most absurd belief in a human without them noticing. Last quarter, Snibber convinced his man that the Enemy's command to "love your neighbor" was really just a call to be polite when convenient. The man now boasts about his "ministry of kindness" while refusing to inconvenience himself for anyone. It's not just effective – it's art.

Apply similar brushstrokes to Elliot. Let him think he's living by the Enemy's truth while quietly swapping pieces of it for counterfeits. Replace "forgive" with "move on." Replace "serve" with "help when it fits your schedule." Replace "trust" with "feel positive about." By the time we're done, he'll be quoting the Book fluently without meaning a word of it.

One final piece of advice; truth corrosion works best when it's reinforced by the heard. Make sure Elliot surrounds himself with people who agree with his diluted definitions.
If a more faithful voice tries to speak up, cast them as judgmental or "too intense." Peer pressure, dear boy, is not just for teenagers; it's for anyone too afraid to stand alone. And if you've done your work right, Elliot will be terrified of standing alone – because alone is where the Enemy's voice is loudest.

By the time you've mastered this with him, you won't need to distract him with shiny objects or weigh him down with endless tasks. He will walk himself away from the Enemy simply because the path no longer looks like the truth to him. And all we had to do was tilt the map a few degrees.

Do not fail me in this. I want to see, in your next report, signs that Elliot's convictions have softened at the edges, that he speaks of truth only in terms of preference, and that he has begun to roll his eyes – even internally – when someone insists the Enemy's words mean exactly what they say. When that happens, dear

Pipwick, you can start planning his slow drift into irrelevance.

Quaver

Yours in persistent subversion,

Quaver
Senior Associate Tempter
Infernal Department of Soul Acquisition
ffice 6B, Third Circle Annex, Central Pit C

FROM THE DESK OF:

QUAVER

SENIOR ASSOCIATE TEMPTER
OFFICE 6B, THIRD CIRCLE ANNEX
CENTRAL PIT COMPLEX

My Dearest Pipwick,

If you ever wish to graduate beyond the rank of "mild inconvenience" to the Enemy's work, you must learn to keep humans obedient in form while rebellious in essence. Outright defiance is flashy but dangerous – it tends to draw His attention like blood in the water. But the quiet, smiling refusal to obey, dressed up as agreement? Ah, that is the marrow of our art.

Your first task in this vein is to convince Elliot that obedience is optional – but never say it outright. Humans know the Enemy is supposed to be their Lord; they've heard the word "command" far too often. What we want is for him to reframe commands as suggestions, or better yet, as lofty ideals that are beautiful to admire but unrealistic to practice. Turn them into wall art – hung up, quoted, but never actually lived.
There is a delightful technique we call the nod-and-ignore. It's very simple.

When Elliot hears something, he knows is true and binding, prompt him to nod solemnly – "Yes, that's good" – and then immediately think of someone else who should apply it. This works brilliantly in sermons. He hears a call to forgive; he nods; he thinks of how his brother-in-law really needs to hear this. He leaves church warmed by agreement but untouched by application.

It's also worth making obedience feel like an interruption. Humans like to imagine themselves as captains of their own time. If you can frame the Enemy's commands as inconvenient to the flow of Elliot's plans, you will subtly make Him seem like a nuisance. Picture this: Elliot feels the nudge to call a lonely friend, but you remind him of the errands waiting. "Do it later," you whisper. Later, of course, never arrives. Over time, the Enemy's voice becomes background noise – always present, never urgent.

Another angle is to load obedience with delay. If you can convince Elliot that following through "when the time is right" is just as good as following through now, you have won the moment. The Enemy delights in immediate obedience; we thrive on postponed obedience, because postponed obedience is almost indistinguishable from disobedience in effect. And the human rarely notices the difference.

Do not neglect the power of partial compliance. Humans are comforted by doing some of what they're told, especially if it's the part they already wanted to do. If Elliot feels prompted to reconcile with someone, encourage him to "pray about it" for a few weeks – this sounds spiritual while keeping him from actually making the call. Or let him send a text instead of meeting face-to-face. He'll check the mental box – "Done" – while the real work remains untouched.

This reminds me of a case handled by Vixlar, who nearly bungled a man ripe for our keeping. The Enemy had told his man – quite clearly – to give away a certain sum of money. Vixlar cleverly convinced him to donate half the amount and tell himself he'd give the rest "when the budget allowed." That "when" never came. By the time the man realized it, years had passed, and the moment was gone. What makes this so delicious is that the man still told the story as a testimony to his generosity. That, Pipwick, is how you turn obedience into an ego boost.

Speaking of ego, always connect obedience to feelings. If Elliot believes he must "feel led" before he obeys, you can keep him paralyzed for weeks. Make him wait for peace before doing hard things; make him wait for motivation before doing costly things. The Enemy often asks for obedience when feelings are dragging behind –

but if you can make feelings the engine rather than the caboose, the train will rarely leave the station.

One of my favorite tools is spiritual busywork. Give him tasks that feel like obedience but require no sacrifice. Let him spend an afternoon designing a "vision board" for how he'll serve others, instead of actually knocking on his neighbor's door. Let him join three church committees that meet monthly but accomplish nothing. Humans love meetings – they smell of purpose while reeking of delay.

Also, be sure to foster the habit of bargaining. When the Enemy asks for something, Elliot doesn't want to give, have him offer something else instead. The Enemy says, "Speak the truth here," and Elliot replies – in his head – I'll give extra in the offering this week." This transactional thinking keeps obedience negotiable. It turns the Enemy into a vendor rather than a King.

And Pipwick, never underestimate the power of redefining terms. If the Enemy commands kindness, make Elliot believe kindness is simply being polite. If the Enemy calls for purity, let him think it means avoiding the really scandalous stuff while indulging in small compromises. Shrink the definitions until they fit comfortably in his existing habits. This way, he can declare victory without ever changing.

In all this, avoid triggering guilt strong enough to drive him to confession. A vague sense of "I should do better" is perfect; it keeps him uneasy but inactive. Strong conviction may drive him straight to the Enemy, and we don't want that. Keep his discomfort mild – like a draft under the door, just enough to make him pull the blanket tighter without getting up to fix it.

Oh, I must tell you about Blither, one of the more creatively incompetent tempters we've had. His man was in the habit of reading the Book each morning. Blither decided to attack the habit directly, which, as I've told you, is the fastest way to make a human dig in his heels. The man actually increased his reading time out of spite. If Blither had been subtle, he could have kept the reading but drained it of power – perhaps buy making the man rush through to get to "the real work" of the day. Always remember: leave the form, stop the power.

Another strategy you should employ is to attach obedience to public perception. If Elliot thinks of obedience mainly as something visible, he will focus on actions that can be applauded. He will avoid the secret acts of faith that no one sees – the ones the Enemy seems to prize most.

Praise that can be measured will always compete with obedience that costs.

And don't forget to make the Enemy's commands seem negotiable based on circumstances. Encourage thoughts like, "I know I should, but this week Is just so busy," or "I'll start after things calm down." The Enemy has a most irritating habit of asking for obedience in inconvenient seasons: your job is to convince Elliot that He surely wouldn't mind if it waited.

Finally, keep obedience abstract. Let Elliot talk about "living for God" without ever identifying a single concrete action he must take today. Abstractions are safe; specifics are dangerous. If the Enemy says, "Apologize," drown it in talk about "fostering unity." If He says, "Give that," wrap it in generalities about "being generous in spirit." He'll feel holy while staying exactly the same.

If you follow these instructions, Pipwick, you will cultivate a man who agrees with the Enemy on paper, nods in all the right places, even prays the right words – but whose feet never move in the direction he's told to go. And the sweetest part? He'll never think of himself as disobedient. He'll call himself "balanced," "thoughtful," or "waiting on God's timing." And by the time he realizes that delayed obedience was disobedience all along, the opportunities will be long past.

Do report back with details of how you've blurred the lines for him. I want to hear of prompts ignored, nudges postponed, and actions replaced with comfortable substitutes, If you can get him to measure his obedience by intention rather than execution, you will have done me proud.

Quaver

Yours in persistent subversion,

Quaver
Senior Associate Tempter
Infernal Department of Soul Acquisition
ffice 6B, Third Circle Annex, Central Pit C

FROM THE DESK OF:

QUAVER

SENIOR ASSOCIATE TEMPTER
OFFICE 6B, THIRD CIRCLE ANNEX
CENTRAL PIT COMPLEX

My Dear Pipwick,

You have been far too soft on Elliot's failures,
You treat the like unfortunate little accidents to
be brushed away, when in reality they are the
most fertile soil we have. Every stumble, every
misstep, every compromise is a seed – and If you
cultivate it properly, it will grow into a vine that
winds itself around his thoughts and chokes the
Enemy's life from him.

Your problem, dear boy, is that you still think
failure is an end in itself. It is not. It is a doorway.
The Enemy, maddeningly, has a habit of barging
through that doorway to drag His people back to
their feet, wipe their faces, and send them on
their way stronger than before. We cannot
prevent Him from doing this outright – but we
can delay it. And in the real of souls, delay is
often as effective as defeat.

The key is to keep Elliot's gaze fixed on the
failure itself rather than on the way back.

If you can make him stare at what he's done until it's the only thing he can see, the path home will grow dim in his mind. Begin the moment he trips; whisper that he's ruined everything, that this is the real him, the truth finally unmasked. Repeat it until it becomes a refrain. Shame is an exquisite sedative when administered in regular doses.

Now, you mustn't overdo the shame. Too much, too fast, and he may run straight to the Enemy for relief. Instead, let it simmer. Keep it low and constant, like the hum of a refrigerator – always there, never loud enough tot wake him fully. This way, every attempt at prayer will feel slightly hollow, every act of service tinged with "you don't deserve to be here." If you mange this correctly, he will still go through the motions while quietly believing he is unworthy of the Enemy's attention.

One of the most effective tools here is the highlight reel. At opportune moments, play back his past failures in vivid color. Make him relive the awkward phrasing of that conversation, the look on someone's face when he disappointed them, the choice he wish he could undo. Humans can replay a thirty-second failure for thirty years if you keep the image sharp.

The trick is to do this right before he tries something new. Ambition shrivels quickly when the mind is full of old embarrassments.

This is where guilt comes in. I must emphasize, Pipwick, that guilt in its raw form is dangerous to us – the Enemy designed it as a warning light, meant to drive them toward Him. Our job is to require it so that guilt drives Elliot away from the very place it's meant to send him. You do this by turning guilt into identity. Instead of "I did something wrong," you feed him "I am the sort of person who does this kind of wrong."

Once you've planted that thought, water it with self-pity. This is a vastly underused weapon among the tempters. Self-pity takes guilt – which might be resolved – and turns it into a treasured possession. "No one knows how hard this is for me," he'll think. "If they did, they wouldn't expect so much." From there, every command of the Enemy becomes negotiable.

Let me tell you a cautionary tale about Murl, one of our more dim-witted colleagues. He had a human who stumbled in a fairly public way – the sort of failure that attracts whispered conversations in hallways. Murl pounced with every ounce of shame he could muster, and the man, crushed by the weight of it, confessed openly, repented, and became a blazing example of restored humility. Murl was transferred the following week. The lesson? Never give them the sort of guilt that forces a decision. Give them just enough to make them avoid the Enemy's presence without quite knowing why.

In Elliot's case, the most promising avenue is to make him compare his failures to those of others. When someone else stumbles, let him notice how much worse they seem. This will give him little jolts of self-righteousness to dull the sting of his own guilt – which means it will never be resolved. Conversely, when he fails, make sure he notices how much better others seem to be doing. That will feed the "I'm hopeless" narrative. Either comparison will do; the goal is to keep his gaze horizontal, never vertical.

Another excellent tactic is the spiritual ledger. Convince Elliot that every failure sets him back to zero in the Enemy's eyes. Let him think of the Christian life as a game of building up credits through good behavior – credits that evaporate instantly when he sins. This way, each failure feels catastrophic, undoing weeks or months of "progress." The exhaustion this creates is marvelous; eventually, he will conclude it's not worth trying.

I recommend adding a touch of perfectionism to the recipe. If you can make him believe the Enemy expects flawless execution, then every imperfect attempt become another failure in his mind. Soon he will prefer not to attempt anything at all rather than risk falling short. Humans call this "playing it safe." We call it "voluntary paralysis."

Do not ignore the small, almost invisible failures – the ones he's tempted to shrug off. A harsh word spoken in irritation, a minor lapse in honesty, a thoughtless promise he never kept – collect these like beads on a string. A lone, each is trivial; together they can be presented to him as proof that he is fundamentally unreliable. And since these failures are small, he will rarely bother to confess them, allowing them to accumulate quietly.

One of my personal favorites is to make him confess without change. Let him say the words – even feel a momentary relief – but never actually address the habit that caused the failure. Over time, confession becomes a soothing ritual rather than a turning point. This hollows it out beautifully, until he is essentially apologizing to the Enemy for sport.

If Elliot beings to recover from a failure, your job is not necessarily to drag him back into the same sin. That can be messy. Instead, turn his recovery into a source of pride. Let him think, "I've overcome that; I'm stronger now." Feed him compliments from others about how well he's "handled" it. If you do this well, the pride will rot him from the inside, and he'll be even less prepared for the next temptation.

You might also consider introducing what we call defensive theology. This is where the human starts crafting beliefs specifically to make himself feel better about his failures. For instance, if the Enemy calls him to holiness, whisper that "God understands" and therefore no real change is necessary. Or twist the Enemy's mercy into an indulgence – "I can always be forgiven" – so that disobedience becomes less alarming.

Let me share a particularly elegant example from Crath, one of the most competent tempters in our ranks. His human was caught in a cycle of dishonesty at work. Rather than push for bigger lies, Crath kept the lies small but constant, all the while feeding the idea that "nobody's perfect."

Over years, the man's moral compass adjusted so subtly that he could no longer recognize dishonesty as wrong unless it was criminal. By then, of course, he was ours in all but paperwork.

For Elliot, I suggest blending two approaches: the mild cloud and the private indulgence. The mild cloud is that low-grade shame I mentioned earlier – a constant sense that he's not quiet measuring up, The private indulgence is the thing he does in secret to "cope" with that feeling. It doesn't even have to be particularly scandalous; the point is that he must believe he can't live without it. The indulgence will reinforce the shame, and the shame will send him back to the indulgence. This loop can run indefinitely without intervention.

Finally, and this is crucial, you must teach him to hidden. Not just from others, but from himself. Let him avoid thinking too deeply about his motives. Keep him busy with surface-level self-improvement, the kind that looks good in conversation but never touches the deeper currents. The Enemy delights in bringing things into the light; our task is to keep them comfortably in the half-shadows, where they can fester without stinking enough to draw attention.

When you master this, Pipwick, you will find that you no longer have to invent temptations for Elliot. His own unresolved failures will keep him in our camp quite nicely. He will smile, attend services, even speak the Enemy's name – but deep inside, he will carry the quiet conviction that he's a disappointment. And a man who believes that will never run boldly into the Enemy's arms.

Report back to me with specifics: the failures you've highlighted, the guilt you've shaped into identity, the delays you've introduced into his repentance. I expect to see evidence of a man who, on the surface, appears unchanged – but whose soul is slowly bending under the weight of a burden he doesn't realize he's carrying.

Quaver

Yours in persistent subversion,

Quaver
Senior Associate Tempter
Infernal Department of Soul Acquisition
ffice 6B, Third Circle Annex, Central Pit C

INFERNAL DEPARTMENT OF
SOUL ACQUISITION

SUB-DIVISION: MID-TIER HUMAN ACCOUNTS
INTERNAL CORRESPONDENCE — LEVEL Ω

FROM THE DESK OF:

QUAVER

SENIOR ASSOCIATE TEMPTER
OFFICE 6B, THIRD CIRCLE ANNEX
CENTRAL PIT COMPLEX

My Dear Pipwick,

I have reviewed your latest updates with something resembling relief – not because you've done brilliantly, but because you haven't yet ruined anything beyond repair. Elliot remains dutiful, attending his little gatherings, even engaging in the Enemy's Book with occasional enthusiasm. To the untrained eye, this might look like defeat for us. To the experienced, it is simply the raw material for our most reliable masterpiece: an industrious but impotent human.

The greatest trick you can pull now is to convince Elliot that activity equal effectiveness. You see, the Enemy has the infuriating habit of measuring worth in terms of faithfulness and hidden fruit – things which often look slow, quiet, and unimpressive.
Our advantage lies in their tendency to measure worth in visible motion. If it looks busy, they think it must be good.

Being wit his schedule. Fill it to the brim with things that have a faint whiff of spirituality but little lasting value. Let him attend planning meetings that lead to nothing. Urge him to volunteer for projects that exist solely to produce reports about themselves. The more he feels the relief of themselves. The more he feel the relief of "I've done something," the less he will notice that nothing has actually been accomplished.

There is an exquisite balance you must strike: keep him busy enough to be tired, but not so overextended that he collapses and reassess his priorities. A constantly tired human is wonderfully malleable – his prayers get shorter, his thoughts lazier, his convictions fuzzier. Yet he must also feel that his tiredness is proof of holiness, so he wears it like a badge.

We call this the martyrdom of the mildly overcommitted. The Enemy calls it folly. Either way, it is one of our most dependable tools.

Do not focus solely on external commitments; you must also fragment his attention internally. When he sits down to read the Book, supply him with little mental reminders of all the things he "must" get done today. Make him feel that the time he spends there is stolen time.

Let him bargain with himself – "I'll just read a verse or two, then I'll get to the list." If you repeat this often enough, the reading becomes a token, the prayers perfunctory, and his mind trains itself to think of devotion as a box to tick rather than a place to dwell.

One of our most deliciously effective tactics is what I call the Treadmill of Good Intentions. Humans adore the sensation of "meaning to do" something virtuous. Thinking about doing it, talking about doing it, even writing it on a list – these can produce nearly the same warm feelings as actually doing it. Encourage Elliot to make grand plans for serving, learning, giving – but always in ways that keep the execution just out of reach. A well-fed intention is a marvelous substitute for obedience.

Let me pause to warn you about an error made by my late colleague Frint. His man was deeply involved in church leadership, always attending events and meetings. Frint assumed he was safely ensnared in the busyness trap and stopped paying close attention. Unfortunately, one of those meetings accidentally turned into a genuine moment of prayer,
in which the man realized how little of his time was being spent on direct obedience. He resigned half of his roles and began spending his mornings in actual communion with the Enemy.

Frint's reassignment was...unpleasant. The lesson? Monitor even the "safe" activities, the Enemy can invade anywhere if left unguarded.

For Elliot, you should season his busyness with just enough recognition from others to make it addictive. Humans will endure almost any level of exhaustion for the sake of being seen as dependable. When someone praises his "servant heart," let him glow a little longer than usual. That glow will keep him saying yes to everything, even when his private life is crumbling.

Now, about that private life: keep his home time shallow. If you can fill his evenings with scrolling, light entertainment, and vague half-conversations, he will have neither the energy nor the clarity to reflect on deeper matters. The goal is not necessarily to corrupt him with scandalous sin – though that is always welcome – but to make him so spiritually anemic that he poses no threat.

One of the best ways to achieve this is to conflate spiritual activity with spiritual growth. Let him believe that every event he attends automatically makes him "more mature." If he joins a Bible study, keep the discussions lively but unfocused, always circling around interesting but irrelevant details. Let them debate translations, argue about ancient customs, or dissect obscure passages without ever asking what the Enemy might require of them in their daily lives. The mind will be occupied; the soul will remain unchanged.

Pipwick, I cannot overstate how important it is to keep him surrounded by others who are equally busy and equally fruitless. Isolation is risky – in solitude, humans sometimes hear the Enemy more clearly. But so is company with truly vibrant believers, who might expose his hollowness. Your ideal setting for him is a crowd of well-meaning but stagnant people, where the unspoken agreement is that no one pushes too hard.

I remember a particularly satisfying case handled by Zern, who kept his man in a flurry of youth ministry events for nearly a decade. There were retreats, endless planning sessions. Not once in all those years did the man actually sit down with one of the youth to hear their story, challenge their faith, or walk with them through a hard season. But oh, the photos he posted! Always smiling, always busy, always doing "the work." When he finally realized the shallowness of it all, his cynicism was so thick that he quit everything – including the few things that might have mattered. That, Pipwick, is the long game.

For Elliot, you must also ensure that he rarely, if ever, asks the Enemy whether he should be doing something. Encourage him to assume that any opportunity presented to him is automatically a calling. The more he says yes without reflection, the less likely he is to recognize when the Enemy's voice is missing from the invitation.

If he ever does begin to question his busyness, your task is to frame that doubt as selfishness. Whisper that slowing down would mean letting people down, abandoning the team, or shirking responsibility. Make him feel that to rest would be to sin. Humans have a strange capacity to turn exhaustion into a virtue, and if you fan that flame, he will gladly burn himself out for causes that have nothing to do with the Enemy's kingdom.

Another angle worth developing is the displacement of priorities. Let him feel spiritually satisfied because he attends a prayer breakfast, even though he hasn't spoken a sincere word to the Enemy in private for weeks. Or let him pour hours into preparing for a service project while ignoring the unresolved tension with his wife. If you keep the external projects polished, the internal decay can proceed unnoticed.

When possible, tie his identity to the busyness itself. Let him think of himself as "the reliable one," "the one people can count on." This identity becomes a chain – he will feel compelled to maintain it even when he senses it is draining him. The more his sense of worth is tied to being needed, the more you can control him simply by supplying a steady stream of needs.

And finally, Pipwick, keep him from never asking the most dangerous question: "Am I actually bearing fruit?" The Enemy measures fruit in transformed lives, in obedience, in love that costs something. We measure it in exhaustion without progress, in projects without purpose, in a calendar that looks impressive but produces nothing that will last. If Elliot begins to suspect the difference, flood him with new opportunities before he has time to examine the old ones.

If you do all this well, he will reach the end of his life with the pleasant illusion that he has been terribly busy for the Enemy – while having accomplished almost nothing of eternal value. And the best part? He will only realize it after it is too late to change.

Report back to me once his calendar is sufficiently clogged and his heart sufficiently empty. I expect to see a man whose hands are always moving, whose mind is always occupied, and whose soul is quietly starving.

Quaver

Yours in persistent subversion,

Quaver
Senior Associate Tempter
Infernal Department of Soul Acquisition
ffice 6B, Third Circle Annex, Central Pit C

FROM THE DESK OF:

QUAVER

SENIOR ASSOCIATE TEMPTER
OFFICE 6B, THIRD CIRCLE ANNEX
CENTRAL PIT COMPLEX

My Dearest Pipwick,

I can almost hear the note of alarm in your last update. You report that Elliot seemed "moved" during last weeks gathering, and you are concerned it might signal a turning point. Oh, dear boy – this is not cause for panic. A flicker of emotion means nothing if you know how to smother it properly. In fact, with the right handling, those little spikes of feeling can become some of our most effective tools.

Humans are peculiarly fond of emotional stirrings. They mistake the swell of the heart, the prickling at the eyes, for deep transformation. If you can train Elliot to confuse conviction with catharsis, you will have him forever chasing the feeling of closeness to the Enemy without ever arriving there. It's rather like encouraging a starving man to watch cooking shows – all the sensation of a meal, none of the substance. The trick is to let the emotion rise – sometimes even encourage it – and then divert it before it produces any concrete change. For example, if he feel convicted about neglecting prayer, let him resolve to "do better" without specifying what that means. The vague intention will soothe the discomfort, and by morning he will have forgotten all about it.

Another reliable tactic is to have him express his conviction prematurely. If he hears something that stirs him, make him share it on social media immediately, perhaps with touching quote or verse. The praise from friends will provide the reward his brain was seeking, and the need to act on the conviction will diminish. They call it "accountability"; we call it "premature applause."

You must also learn to harness the social dynamics of these gatherings. If Elliot experiences a moment of conviction while surrounded by others, feed him subtle comparisons. Let him notice those who are visibly moved and feel pleased that he is not "as emotional" as they are – or, conversely, let him notice those who seem unaffected and feel superior for being "more in tune." Either form of comparison will shift his focus from the Enemy's voice to the social atmosphere, which is exactly where we want it.
One of the most delicious methods is to convert conviction into pride. Yes, pride!

It's far simpler than you might think. When Elliot senses the Enemy's prompting, whisper that this shows how mature he's become. Let him mentally pat himself on the back for "still being sensitive" after all these years. In time, he will learn to seek the pleasure of being the sort of person who is convicted, rather than the discomfort of actually obeying the conviction.

I recall the exquisite case of Snerf, who once kept a man in a perpetual loop of "personal revival." Every few months the man would be swept up in some spiritual high, convinced that this time he was truly changed. He would give stirring testimonies, receive warm congratulations, and bask in the glow of being "on fire." And then, quietly, the fire would fade – until the next stirring. Over decades, he learned to crave the cycle itself, and the Enemy never got more than a few weeks of genuine obedience out of him at a time. Snerf was commended for artistry.

You must also blunt the edge of conviction through distraction. Humans are remarkably adept at losing their train of thought. If Elliot feels a pang about his temper, quickly remind him of an unrelated task – an email he must send, a bill he forgot to pay.
If he's in the middle of a sermon, plant a sudden memory of that odd remark his coworker made

yesterday. The mind can only hold one thread at a time with full attention; give him another to tug, and the Enemy's thread will slip away.

Another subtle maneuver is to let him act on conviction in a way that is entirely safe. Suppose he feels prompted to reconcile with someone. Before he has time to consider an actual conversation, suggest he pray a quick, generic prayer for them instead. Or if he feels he should be more generous, have him drop a small amount of change into a charity box – enough to quiet the conscience, too little to cost him anything. The Enemy desires sacrifices, we prefer token gestures.

One of my personal favorites is to encourage him to "prepare" indefinitely. If he feels called to serve in some capacity, make him believe he must first read three books on the subject, attend a seminar, and spend weeks "seeking confirmation." By the time he has completed these preparatory steps, the initial spark will have gone cold, and he will feel strangely relieved not to have committed.

Of course, there is also the simple art of delay. Conviction loses much of its potency when left to sit.

Encourage Elliot to tell himself, "I'll start tomorrow" – or better yet, "after the weekend" or "when things settle down." Humans are fond of imagining that their future selves will be braver, kinder, and more obedient than they are today. We must never let them notice that tomorrow's self is just today's self with less time.

When Elliot does act on a conviction, make it hurried and ill-considered. The Enemy often works slowly, deliberately; we can ruin much by rushing. Let him attempt to apologize without listening, to give without thought, to speak without preparation. A botched obedience can be worse than none at all, for it leaves a sour taste in the mouth and makes him wary of trying again.

If at any point you sense that he is on the verge of sustained change, bring up his past failures. Remind him how may time he has "started fresh" only to end up back where he began. Suggest that the Enemy must be tired of hearing the same promises. Let him think that real change is impossible – that conviction is merely the Enemy's way of toying with him. The resulting hopelessness will be a balm to us and a wall between him and help.

Now, a word of emotional highs.

They are not always dangerous; indeed, they can be quite useful if you ensure they remain isolated from daily life. Let Elliot believe that the Enemy's presence is primarily experienced in special moments – at conferences, during moving music, in dramatic circumstances. Then, when ordinary days come) as they inevitably do), he will feel that the Enemy is absent. This will either lead to boredom, which we can exploit, or to a restless search for the next "spiritual hit," which keeps him from the steady, quiet obedience the Enemy so values.

I must caution you, however, against allowing him to despise emotion altogether. That can drive him toward a cold, rigid obedience which, while lacking warmth, can still be effective for the Enemy. Far better to let him cherish emotion but treat it as the main course rather than the appetizer. Keep him busy chasing feelings, and he will never notice that his faith is an inch deep.

An anecdote to illustrate: Vrank once oversaw a woman who loved the Enemy's music. She felt closest to Him while singing in the assembly. Vrank subtly taught her to equate that feeling with spiritual health. When she eventually lost her voice to illness, she believed she had lost her faith entirely. She drifted into bitterness within months.

All it took was convincing her that the emotional expression was the substance. You would do well to remember this principle.

In Elliot's case, I recommend a mixture of tactics: allow him moments of stirring, but always follow them with diversion, token action, or pride. Let him talk about how "convicted" he feels; let him even make small, symbolic changes – rearranging his schedule, buying a new devotional book, perhaps. But never let those changes reach the root of his habits.

To maintain this state, surround him with others who reinforce it. People who also equate emotion with depth, who applaud public expressions but rarely ask private questions. The social reinforcement will be invaluable; no one wants to be the only one in the room asking, "But what will we do about it?"

Finally, Pipwick, learn to savor the long-term effects of this strategy. A human who has lived years in the illusion of responsiveness is wonderfully resistant to genuine transformation. He will have trained himself to feel satisfied at the first twinge of conviction, so that when the Enemy calls him to something costly, he will feel no urgency. "I've already responded," he will think – and he will mean that he felt something, perhaps said something, but never did anything.

That is the kind of soul we want: stirred, but not changed; active, but not obedient; full of impressions, but empty of fruit.

I expect you to keep careful record of every conviction diverted, every moment of clarity turned into self-congratulation, every act of obedience reduced to a token. In time, Elliot will be a man who hears much and does little – and that, dear Pipwick, is victory.

Quaver

Yours in persistent subversion,

Quaver
Senior Associate Tempter
Infernal Department of Soul Acquisition
ffice 6B, Third Circle Annex, Central Pit C

FROM THE DESK OF:

QUAVER

SENIOR ASSOCIATE TEMPTER
OFFICE 6B, THIRD CIRCLE ANNEX
CENTRAL PIT COMPLEX

My Dear Pipwick,

You will be pleased to know that the subtle corrosion we've been working toward has prepared the prefect soil for our next crop: the flexible truth. By "flexible" I mean that variety of truth which bends itself to convenience, preference, and social expedience, all while retaining the appearance of integrity. The Enemy has an irritating fondness for describing truth as unchanging, like some immovable pillar. We prefer something more...accommodating.

Do not attempt to strip Elliot of the concept of truth outright – such work is clumsily and far too likely to awaken suspicion. Instead, being by treating truth as a matter of emphasis. Let him believe that what is technically true can be selectively presented to paint whatever picture is more useful to him.
For instance, if he has a conflict with a colleague, encourage him to share "his side" in ways that leave out inconvenient details.

He will tell himself he is not lying; he is merely "focusing on what matters."

Once you have him comfortable with omission, you may introduce the art of interpretation. Here you must be subtle. Suggest that everyone has their own perspective and that his is just as valid as anyone else's – perhaps more so, given his "experience" or "wisdom." The more he believes that truth is determined by the teller, the easier it will be to detach him from any objective standard.

Encourage him to dress his interpretations in the robes of empathy. If he reframes events to spare someone's feelings, he will think himself kind. If he avoids telling a difficult truth to keep the peace, he will think himself wise. And if he alters a detail here or there to protect his own image, well, surely that's only human. What begins as compassion will quietly evolve into manipulation, and all without the ugly taste of guilt.

This is where your earlier work on his appetite for approval will serve you well. A man who craves affirmation will always be tempted to shape his vision of truth to match the audience.
Let him notice how certain answers make people smile, how certain omissions make him look better. Before long, he will develop an

instinct for tailoring truth in the same way one tailors a suit – trimming off the edges that do not fit.

You must also corrupt his sense of proportion. Not all distortions are equal, but if you can convince him that "little white lies" are harmless, you can gradually expand his tolerance for larger ones. He will tell himself that lying about a missed appointment to avoid embarrassment is no different from lying to spare someone else's feelings. Eventually, the line will blur entirely.

I recall the delightful case of Brinth, who kept his man in a constant state of self-justification by appealing to his identity as a "peacekeeper." The man would omit unpleasant truths in conversations, downplay serious issues, and spin events to maintain harmony. Over time, he became so practiced in selective truth-telling that he could not even admit reality to himself. When the Enemy tried to break through, he had no language left for confession – everything had been reframed until it was harmless. Brinth was promoted.

With Elliot, you should take advantage of his environment. In professional settings, emphasize the value of "managing perceptions." In his social life, focus on "being considerate."

In his faith community, whisper about "avoiding stumbling blocks." All these phrases can be bent to mean "never tell the unvarnished truth if it might cost you." The beauty of this approach is that he will not only deceive others; he will also feel noble doing so.

It is also essential to dismantle the link between truth and trust. The Enemy designed them to be inseparable – truth builds trust, trust strengthens relationships. We, however, can persuade Elliot that relationships are maintained through tact, not honesty. Let him think that if people really knew the whole truth about him, they would reject him. Then, concealment becomes not merely a choice but a survival tactic.

Once he had adopted this mindset, you can feed him small hypocrisies until they no longer feel like compromises. He can speak warmly about generosity while privately resenting every request for help. He can advocate for forgiveness while keeping careful record of every slight. And all the while, he will feel that as long as the words are technically correct, he has maintained integrity.

Do not neglect the opportunity to use his faith language against him. The Enemy's Book contains many warnings about the tongue, but humans are adept at using those same passages to police others rather than themselves. If you can get Elliot to apply "speaking the truth in love" primarily to correcting others while excusing his own evasions, you will have hollowed out his moral compass nicely.

Now, there is more advanced tactics that requires finesse; the "contextual truth." This involves teaching him that what is true in one situation might not be in another – not because the facts change, but because the audience changes. He will tell himself that he is "adapting" or "being relevant," but in reality, he is editing reality itself. Once this habit is formed, the very idea of a single, fixed truth will seem quaint and impractical.

I must warn you against letting this slide into blatant dishonesty too quickly. Humans are curiously defensive of their self-image as "honest people," even when their lives are built on subtle deceit. If you push him into an obvious, undeniable lie before he is ready, you risk awakening his conscience in full.

Far better to keep him in the murky middle ground, where he can tell himself he has never truly lied – only "adjusted" for the circumstances.

A particularly satisfying case involved a young man under my colleague Draff, who learned to give different version of his opinions depending on whether he was with his friend, his boss, or his church group. He thought himself skilled at "connecting" with different kinds of people. By the time he realized he no longer knew what he actually believed, the habit was irreversible. He had become a mirror – reflecting whatever stood in front of him.

To cement this in Elliot, pair it with erosion of his appetite for hard truths. Encourage him to avoid difficult conversations altogether. When someone challenges him, let his mind leap to defensiveness rather than curiosity, If he hears a sermon that touches uncomfortably on one of his habits, remind him of all the people who "needed to hear that more." The Enemy's truth cannot take root in a soil that refuses to be disturbed.

You might also wish to introduce the noble-sounding concept of "balance" – not in its genuine form, which can be healthy, but as an excuse to dilute truth until it offends no one. If a clear statement from the Enemy's Book might cause friction, have him add so many qualifiers and concessions that its meaning is lost. He will feel he is being wise and diplomatic;

in reality, he is smothering the truth under layers of padding.

Do not overlook the role of memory in this campaign. Human recollections are notoriously malleable. If you can prompt him to replay past events in his mind with slight alterations, he will eventually believe his own edits. This is especially effective in matters of guilt; a softened memory makes repentance unnecessary. Over time, his personal history will be a curated museum, displaying only those artifacts that flatter him.

And of course, Pipwick, remember that the ultimate aim is not merely to make him tell lies, but to make him live one. A man who habitually bends truth outward will eventually bend it inward. He will redefine his motives to suit his ego, reframe his failures as misunderstandings, and recast his disobedience as prudence. At that point, he ins nearly untouchable by the Enemy's appeals, for he no longer recognizes the language of reality.

When you reach that stage, you may begin to see the fruits: relationships marked by shallow trust, decisions made for appearances, convictions that shift with the wind. And best of all, he will still think of himself as a fundamentally honest man. That, dear Pipwick, is the triumph – not in open deceit, which can be spotted and corrected, but in the hidden distortion, which becomes invisible to the one practicing it. Guard this work carefully If the Enemy gets even a sliver of genuine truth past the defenses, it can unravel years of our efforts. But if you keep him in this flexible, situational approach long enough, he will reach the point where the very idea of absolute truth feels foreign, even threatening. Then he will be ours in mind as well as in deed.

Report back once you have secured his comfort with omission, shaped his reflexes toward tailoring truth, and dulled his appetite for reality unfiltered. At that point, we may move to the next phase – where truth is not just bent, but optional.

Quaver

Yours in persistent subversion,

Quaver
Senior Associate Tempter
Infernal Department of Soul Acquisition
flice 6B, Third Circle Annex, Central Pit C

FROM THE DESK OF:

QUAVER

SENIOR ASSOCIATE TEMPTER
OFFICE 6B, THIRD CIRCLE ANNEX
CENTRAL PIT COMPLEX

My Dear Pipwick,

You will be relieved to know that Elliot's softening toward subjective truth has opened the next door for us: the management of his companions. You see, dear boy, once you've taught a human to bend reality, it become imperative to surround him with people who will not notice – or, better still, who will applaud the skill. This is how you prevent the Enemy from inserting those dreadful "iron-sharpening-iron" types who have the nasty habit of noticing inconsistency and pressing in with awkward questions.

Humans rarely recognize how much of themselves is formed by the company they keep. They imagine themselves as strong, independent thinkers – while unconsciously mirroring the language, priorities, and moral temperature of their nearest associates. If you can shape Elliot's circle, you can shape Elliot.

And you needn't do it by removing all positive influences at once; simply dilute them.

Start with convenience. Encourage him to spend time with those who are easiest to be around – not necessarily the most foolish or corrupt, but the most undemanding. Let him gravitate toward friends who never challenge his decisions, who nod along with his opinions, who would rather change the subject than risk tension. The result will be a pleasant, frictionless environment in which nothing sharpens and nothing grows.

Make sure he avoids sustained contact with anyone who might unsettle him in a productive way. If a co-worker or acquaintance has a habit of asking how his spiritual life is going, ensure their schedules never align. A "too busy" calendar is an excellent tool for this; even the Enemy's best emissaries cannot influence someone they never see.

Next, plant in him a mild suspicion of anyone who seems "too intense" about their convictions. That way, even if such a person enters his orbit, he will keep them at arm's length. The suspicion needn't be overt; a subtle distaste will suffice. Whisper to him that people who talk too much about the Enemy are probably compensating for something, or that they're trying to be "holier-than-thou."

Once he has a category in his mind for "overly spiritual people," you can place any inconvenient voice into it and dismiss them wholesale.

Your work in twisting his desire for approval will come in handy here as well. Make him increasingly dependent on the warmth of his chosen group's acceptance, so that the thought of displeasing them becomes unpleasant enough to stifle dissent. This will keep him from introducing challenging topics or disagreeing with the group consensus. Social comfort is one of the Enemy's greatest gifts – but only when tethered to truth. Sever that tether, and it becomes one of our finest sedatives.

Be sure to curate his digital world as well. It is no longer necessary to isolate a man physically when you can isolate him algorithmically. Steer his online habits toward communities, pages, and personalities that mirror his own biases back at him. Once his feeds are a consistent echo chamber, he will come to believe that "everyone" sees the world the way he does – and any dissent will feel not only wrong, but alien.

You might wonder, dear boy, whether such homogeneity will make him suspicious. Fear not. Humans are curiously flattered by agreement. He will mistake uniformity for unity, and by the time he realizes he has stopped encountering contrary voices, he will also have lost the appetite for them.

Now, here's the delicious side effect: as his circle shrinks in challenge but grows in affirmation, he will also begin to project this dynamic onto the Enemy. He will come to expect that the Enemy's voice will always comfort, never confront. When a passage from the Enemy's Book does confront him, he will assume it has been "misinterpreted" or "taken out of context" – because surely, his God would never say something that makes him uncomfortable. This is how the slow narrowing of human relationships can lead to the slow narrowing of divine authority.

Let me share a little case history for your instruction. My associate Grev once oversaw a woman whose early life has been surrounded by people of diverse conviction – some irritatingly firm, others troublingly compassionate. Grev gradually arranged her circumstances so that she interacted almost exclusively with those who validated her every decision. Over the years, she lost the ability to process disagreement without offense. Eventually, even the Enemy's Spirit, when speaking through her own conscience, was dismissed as "negativity."

Grev did not need to win arguments; he simply removed them.

You must also encourage Elliot to view relationships transactionally. This ensures that he will naturally gravitate toward those who offer the greatest return for the smallest investment. If someone challenges him but offers no immediate benefit in career or reputation, they will quietly drop down his list of priorities. If someone flatters him or provides useful connections, they will move up. The calculus will feel entirely reasonable to him – he is, after all, "managing his energy" and "protecting his peace."

An important maintenance task is to prevent reconciliation in strained relationships that could serve as conduits for the Enemy's influence. If he has had a falling out with someone whose voice carried weight in his life, keep the rift alive. A quiet grudge is a wonderful barrier. Feed him just enough irritation to avoid reaching out, and enough pride to expect the other person to make the first move. Over time, the memory of the person's good influence will fade, leaving only the sting of the conflict.

Do not underestimate the role of humor in cementing group norms.

If you can get Elliot and his companions to regularly joke about the same targets – particularly those who live with a seriousness about the Enemy's commands – you will have turned peer pressure into a reflex. No one wants to be the subject of the group's ridicule, so Elliot will instinctively avoid the behaviors and beliefs that attract it.

It is equally useful to encourage relationships built entirely on shared complaints. These can be intoxicatingly bonding, as humans find solidarity in mutual grievances. The more Elliot bonds with others over what they dislike, the less energy he will have for anything that requires risk, forgiveness, or growth. And because the complaints will usually be about other people, you will have the added benefit of keeping his focus horizontal rather than vertical.

A particularly elegant touch is to exploit nostalgia. Encourage him to idolize past relationships that were lighthearted and non-demanding, and to measure new ones by that impossible standard. This will make deeper, more challenging connections feel heavy or disappointed by comparison. Nostalgia is a sly way of making the present seem inadequate without having to justify why.

Once Elliot's social diet is sufficiently curated, you can start using it to reinforce other distortions. His approval-seeking will be rewarded by the echo chamber. His subjective truth will be echoed back at him as wisdom. Even his occasional pangs of conscience will be met with well-meaning reassurances that he is "too hard on himself." Slowly, the circle becomes self-policing – any intrusion by the Enemy will be met not only by Elliot's defenses, but the defenses of those around him.

Now, do not imagine this work will remain static. Humans change – they move cities, switch jobs, lose touch. You must be vigilant in replacing lost influences with suitable equivalents. A single season of exposure to a challenging friendship can undo years of our labor if the man is allowed to dwell in it. Always be watching for the stray invitation, the unexpected reconnection, the inconvenient mentor. Smother these with scheduling conflicts, petty misunderstandings, or the vague feeling that "Iti would be awkward."

In rare cases, you may even have to work with the material the Enemy provides. If Elliot does befriend someone inconveniently committed to truth and love, encourage the relationship to remain superficial. Let them exchange pleasantries, laugh about harmless topics, maybe even share a few personal anecdotes – but never let them reach the depth where genuine influence happens. This can be accomplished by ensuring that most of their time together is in groups, where conversation stays safe and general.

One final caution: never allow him to realize how small his world has become. If he does, the shock might drive him to see out broader, healthier connections. Keep him busy enough that the lack of diversity in his relationships feels like stability rather than stagnation.

Once this structure is in place, the Enemy will find it nearly impossible to insert the kind of truth-bearing voices that threaten our cause. And even if one slips through, the surrounding circle will quickly neutralize it. Elliot will have become a man surrounded by comforters, shielded from challenges – a perfect greenhouse for slow, steady ruin.

Guard this arrangement well, Pipwick. A man's companions are like the air he breathes; poison it gently, and he will never notice until it's far too late.

Quaver

Yours in persistent subversion,

Quaver
Senior Associate Tempter
Infernal Department of Soul Acquisition
ffice 6B, Third Circle Annex, Central Pit C

FROM THE DESK OF:

QUAVER

SENIOR ASSOCIATE TEMPTER
OFFICE 6B, THIRD CIRCLE ANNEX
CENTRAL PIT COMPLEX

CONFIDENTIAL — FOR DEMONIC EYES ONLY
UNAUTHOREIZED READING BY HUMANS WILL ESULT
IN IMMEDIATE DISCIPLINARY REVIEW AND/OR THE
REASSIGNMENT OF YOUR MOST PROMISING CASE
TO THE COMPLAINTS DEPARTMENT.

My Dear Pipwick,

We are entering the delicious phase where Elliot's conscience is pliable, his companions are compliant, and his definition of truth is sufficiently elastic. Now, we must teach him the crowning skill: the rebranding of vice as virtue. This is not merely about doing wrong without guilt; it is about doing wrong while believing it to be right. That, my dear boy, is a far safer prison – for it locks from the inside.

The Enemy, in His frustrating clarity, calls certain things sin and expects His followers to take Him at His word. Our work is to make Elliot believe that what the Enemy calls disobedience can be reinterpreted as wisdom, prudence, or self-care. This is the oldest art in our trade; our Master used it in the very first human conversation: "Did He really say...?" We simply apply modern accents to the same ancient question.

Being small. Take a command Elliot already agrees with in theory – generosity, for example –

and introduce the notion that in his particular circumstances, generosity might be unwise. Remind him of times the recipient strained his resources or when the recipient misused what he gave. Before long, he will begin to see withholdings as stewardship, stinginess as discernment. It is crucial that this shift feels thoughtful, not rebellious.

Next, encourage him to apply this logic to the Enemy's call for reconciliation. Instead of seeing it as a moral imperative, have him view it as an optional act that must be weighed against personal "boundaries" or "emotional safety." He will persuade himself that refusing to forgive is an act of maturity – after all, he is "protecting himself" from further harm. What was once disobedience is now framed as wisdom.

The beauty of this method is that you needn't confront his values head-on. Simply redefine them in practice. Courage becomes reckless; caution becomes cowardice; conviction become stubbornness – all with the Enemy's will or ours. If the Enemy commands boldness, make Elliot think it's wiser to wait. If He commands patience, make Elliot think seizing the moment is the braver course. By swapping the labels, you can have him walking in the opposite direction while congratulating himself for his obedience.

A particularly satisfying tactic is to weaponize his experiences. If he once took risk that failed, file that memory under "reasons to avoid unnecessary risks," even if the failure was due to his own half-heartedness. If he once showed kindness that was exploited, catalog it was evidence that kindness must be "earned." In this way, you transform his scars into guiding principles that conveniently protect him form the Enemy's more demanding instructions.

You will find Elliot's hunger for approval (which we have so carefully cultivated) to be a powerful ally here. Public opinion can be made to masquerade as godly counsel. If his peers praise him for a decision, even when nit contradicts the Enemy's Book, he will feel affirmed. The Enemy's voice will be drowned out by the warm chorus of agreement – and he will call it confirmation.

Do not neglect his prayer life in this stage. It is vital that his prayers remain vague and self-preferential, filled with requests for "peace" and "clarity" but devoid of specific risky obedience. If he begins to suspect that the Enemy is leading him toward something uncomfortable, whisper into his mind that the Enemy would never ask him to do anything "irresponsible." The longer he equates safety with divine will, the more allergic he will become to any call that demands sacrifice.

We once had a man, under my colleague Sern, who had been commanded – by both conscience and clear opportunity – to reconcile with a family member. But Sern whispered that doing so would be "enabling" the other's bad behavior. The man nodded to himself, told a few friends who all agreed, and wen tot his grave convinced that his refusal was a mark of maturity. The family never reconciled. Sern was promoted.

With Elliot, you can accelerate this process by exploiting the language of balance. Have him believe that every virtue, when taken too far, becomes a vice – and then quietly redefine "too far" as "whenever it inconveniences me." This is an especially effective way to tame his generosity, commitment, and honesty. He will be able to tell himself that he values these things, all while never practicing them beyond the threshold of comfort.

Another line of attack is to blur the distinction between motives and results. If Elliot can convince himself that his intentions were good, he will excuse almost any action. This allows you to redirect his decisions toward whatever benefits him most, without him ever having to confront the selfishness of the outcome. The equation is simple: "I meant well" = "I did well."

In his work life, have him cut corners for "efficiency." In his friendships, have him withhold truth to "keep the peace." In his spiritual life, have him skip disciplines for "rest." Over time, the pattern will solidify: whenever the Enemy's commands conflict with his preferences, the preferences will win – dressed in the Enemy's own clothing.

Now, a subtle but potent reinforcement comes from encouraging him to see exceptions as the norm. If a command feels burdensome, have him recall a rare situation where breaking it seemed justified, then elevate that exception into a principle. For example, if once in his youth he lied to spare someone's feelings, and it appeared to do no harm, let him build a moral framework in which lying is not only acceptable but preferably in many situation.

It will also help to keep his life full of half-obedience's. If the Enemy prompts him to help a neighbor in need, let him do the bare minimum and then congratulate himself for his generosity. If called to confront a harmful pattern in himself, let him acknowledge it privately but take no concrete steps to change. Half-measures are excellent for keeping the conscience quiet while preventing any real transformation.

Guard against allowing him to notice this hypocrisy. The moment he suspects that he is explaining away the Enemy's commands, the whole scheme is at risk. Keep his mind occupied with comparing himself to others – particularly those who are openly disobedient. As long as he feels more virtuous than "those people," he will never examine whether his won virtue is merely repackaged vice.

An advance tactic, which I trust you will employ with care, is to feed him stories of people who obeyed the Enemy at great cost and seemed to suffer for it. Twist the moral util it becomes a cautionary tale: "See what happens when you take things too literally? Best to be wise and moderate." Soon, Elliot will avoid the Enemy's most radical calls as if they were traps.

Over time, Pipwick, this redefinition process will create a man who cannot be corrected – not because he refuses correction outright, but because he believes he is already wise. And when a man believes his disobedience is actually obedience, he becomes an evangelist for our cause without ever knowing it. He will teach others to be as "balanced" as he is, spreading the infection while thinking he's offering medicine.

Your goal, then, is not merely to keep him from doing what the Enemy asks, but to make him believe that doing so would be foolish.. When he hears a sermon about sacrifice, he should nod appreciatively and think of someone else who needs to hear it. When he reads a passage about loving enemies, he should agree wholeheartedly – as long as the "enemy" in question is hypothetical.

The final product will be a man who avoids the Enemy's most transformative command without ever admitting that he has disobeyed. He will stand before others, and even before the Enemy Himself, with the serene confidence of one who has lived wisely – when in truth, he has simply lived comfortably.

Do not lose your nerve now, Pipwick. This is the penultimate stage. After this, only one more turn of the screw remains before Elliot is beyond retrieval. Make him a man who wears the Enemy's colors while marching to our drum, and you will have secured a prize worth boasting of in the Lower Halls.

Quaver

Yours in persistent subversion,

Quaver
Senior Associate Tempter
Infernal Department of Soul Acquisition
ffice 6B, Third Circle Annex, Central Pit C

FROM THE DESK OF:

QUAVER

SENIOR ASSOCIATE TEMPTER
OFFICE 6B, THIRD CIRCLE ANNEX
CENTRAL PIT COMPLEX

CONFIDENTIAL — FOR DEMONIC EYES ONLY
UNAUTHOREIZED READING BY HUMANS WILL ESULT
IN IMMEDIATE DISCIPLINARY REVIEW AND/OR THE
REASSIGNMENT OF YOUR MOST PROMISING CASE
TO THE COMPLAINTS DEPARTMENT.

My Dear Pipwick,

You have been remarking in your last few dispatches that our case is "practically finished," a phrase that should never be used by anyone who wishes to keep his job. There is no "practically" about this work, A soul is either turning or it is not, and the Enemy, infuriatingly, can turn a man as quickly as one turns a page. We do not get to count drafts as victories. We only get signatures.

Do not misunderstand me: you have done adequate work. Elliot is lulled by respectable pleasures, preoccupied with his image, coached to prefer flexible truth and low-friction companions.
He has learned to rationalize disobedience as wisdom, to mistake motion for fruit, to equate conviction with catharsis. On paper, this is delightful. In practice, paper catches fire.

I write today because something has shifted, something so small you will be tempted to miss it. It was not a flashing light or a thunderclap (you always watch the horizon and miss what is underfoot). It was a pause. A quiet, stubborn pause – last night, in the kitchen, while the kettle breathed, He meant to scroll (your faithful bell chimed), meant to write a list (your faithful whisper nagged), meant to choose a show (your faithful algorithm wagged its tail). And he…stopped. Only half a breath, barely a measurable unit. But it was the Enemy's kind of stillness, the sort that turns the entire room toward a door you hadn't noticed, the sort that makes every lesser noise embarrassed to be heard.

Do not panic. Do not exult. Take notes.

The pause was not an achievement; it was an opening. He did not spring to his knees, he did not weep, he did not fling away his devices with a vow. He rubbed his eyes and said, aloud, "Lord, I am tired of pretending." That is all. Nine words, and I felt the floor tilt.

Pretending, Pipwick, is our native element, the atmosphere we have so patiently thickened around him. If he can name it – if he can want something truer than his own comfort – you must assume the Enemy is in the room whether or not you smell Him.

Do not rush to smother such moments with loud temptations. That is the novice's mistake. Loudness will only confirm the significance of what happened by contrast. No, work with velvet: errands, small tasks, the polite tug of a notification. Let him forget by inches. If he remembers in the morning only that he "had a moment," and if that memory feels faint enough to fold, we can keep our scaffolding intact.

Unfortunately, he did not forget. He woke with the sentence still forming itself, a stubborn thread he could not tuck away. It followed him into the shower, stood in the hallway as he tied his shoes, rode to work on the passenger seat like an accusation. "Tired of pretending" is a dangerous incantation because it points toward a Shape that is not him. He suspects there is life on the other side of our curtains. He suspects it is not constructed by mood or applause. He suspects – oh, curse this – he suspects it has a King.

At his desk, he did what you have trained him to do: he rewarded his discomfort with busywork. Bless you for that reflex. He cleared emails, arranged meetings, re-labeled folders, answered a call he would normally send to voicemail (an impressive flourish; you see, even we can be surprised by the intricate choreography of our own conditioning). And still the thread tugged.

He found himself opening a document to type the phrase – he did not, thank the Lower Halls, type it. He would not like how plain it looks in black on white. He prefers cleverness. Keep him preferring cleverness. Clever men are allergic to plain things.

After lunch, something miniature but precise intervened: a calendar alert he had set weeks ago to call an old friend who has grown inconveniently earnest. He almost dismissed it. Habit carried his thumb halfway across the screen. Then that stubborn pause returned, as if the morning had only practiced it. He did not call – not yet – but he moved the alert to early evening instead of deleting it. You think this is nothing. It Is not nothing. A man who begins to move temptation into the future rather than immediately burying it is learning the shape of refusal.

You will ask (because you always ask): where did the pause come from?
The answer is both embarrassing and consistent. Yesterday, a child laughed at his attempt to fix a crooked lamp – laughed not unkindly, just delighted at the sight of a grown man muttering at a stubborn screw. He laughed too, and for one moment his competence ceased to be the altar upon which he offered his self-worth. In the crack where dignity stood, air

came through. The Enemy often selects such trivial hammers. We mock them until they break our teeth.

The evening, thankfully, offered you several opportunities to convert recollection into ritual. The cough was loyal. The stream scrolled out is possibilities like a train of silk. He hovered – oh, we know that hover, the little dance at the border. Then the rescheduled call buzzed. He could have ignored it. He answered.

The friend did an unforgiveable thing: he told the truth without polishing it. No sermon, no performance. "I miss you," he said. "You've felt far away." He did not accuse, he did not angle for a promise, he did not throw stones at Elliot's careful excuses. He named the gap and waited inside it as if waiting were a kind of welcome. The Enemy does this, and His allies, when they are not trying to impress one another, sometimes remember.

Elliot did not confess. Calm yourself. He did not pour out secrets we could never stuff back in. He spoke carefully, as befits a man who has learned to protect his image with soft words. But he said something like honesty: " I don't want to keep faking my way through." He did not define the terms. He does not know the depth of the claim. He made it anyway. The friend suggested a small thing – curse him – "Let's read one psalm each morning and text a sentence to each other about what stood out." There it is, Pipwick: specificity. Our entire campaign has aimed at keeping his religion abstract. If he agrees to anything particular, you must crowd the day with fog.

He agreed.

Do not despair. Men agree to may things in the evening they cannot find at dawn. We have made certain that dawn is a cramped room full of wires. Yet I am not writing to soothe you; I am writing because there is a scent in this that I loathe recognizing. It is the smell of a plan smaller than the problem. We cannot outshout a psalm at six in the morning with a thousand shows at nine at night. We must place our hands on the hinge.

I recommend three immediate lines of countermeasure.

First, make the psalm about performance. If he must do this, let him do it competitively. Help him read for cleverness, for the sentence he can text that will sound profound without touching nerve. If he practice yields applause (even polite, friendly applause), he will keep the practice for the wrong reason and miss the Person. I would rather have him faithful to an audience than faithful to a King.

Second, keep the mornings short. Wake him twice in the night with trivial concerns – a bill, a message, a flitting memory of a mistake made years ago (the "highlight reel" remains our evergreen device). When the alarm rings, make the pillow a cathedral. If he rises anyway, let every small noise of the house insist that he is selfish for taking this time. Let the kettle scream, let the dog paw, let the sink drip. If he texts a sentence, let it be clipped. Friction is our friend.

Third, frame the experiment as an improvement, not a surrender. Improvement keeps the ego in charge. Surrender puts a sword into the Enemy's hand. If asked how it is going, let him say, "It's helpful," rather than, "I am being undone." Men continue helpful things until bored. No on continues being undone unless Someone keeps remaking him.

Now to the matter that has been crawling at the edge of my sight since last night. At dinner, his wife said almost nothing and everything. She asked if he might come to bed earlier because she misses him – no the body on the mattress, the man. She did not weep. She set down a fork and looked at him as if the space between them was furniture that could be moved. He tried one of your approved deflections ("busy week," "lots on the go"), and it fell to the floor like cut string. Do not underestimate the Enemy's knack for arranging domestic furniture into altars. A single honest sentence at a table can be burnt offering with smoke that reaches beyond our ceilings.

After the plates, he considered retreat to the couch. He is a master of polite retreat. He did not retreat. He stood beside her at the sink. Their fingers touched in the soap. This is sentimental nonsense, you say. Yes, and the Enemy loves to traffic power in sentimental disguises. Affection is one of the quickest roads to attention, and attention is the gate to obedience. If they remember each other as persons, our screens dim.

I can hear your quill scratching: "But what of all our prior work? Does none of it hold?" Some of it holds very well.

Watch how quickly he reaches for small comforts when the smallest discomfort arrives. See him graze the pantry door, see him negotiate with the evening (one episode, half an hour, we'll still read later). See how eager he is to narrate his intentions instead of living them. Our patterns are not erased by one pause; they are simply challenged. But that challenge is precisely the sort that can teach a man to detest the patterns that have made him thin. The Enemy often turns distaste into discipline.

What is to be done? You will want to file a petition to transfer me this case or you that case. Do not waste bureaucracy on crisis; Administration notices only when we notice. Retain the appearance of routine. We fight this in plain clothes.

Press in every hinge I have named. Make the shared reading logistical: mismatched schedules, misplaced phones, a sudden, totally plausible need to get to the office early. When he texts, let the friend's reply arrive late. The Enemy's timing is perfect; ours must be disruptive. If two mornings pass without the exchange, the third can be skipped with a shrug. "We tried" is one of our sweetest epitaphs.

Leverage the old gods we trained. Approval: remind him subtly that his cleverness has a market. Suggest he post a sentence from the psalm publicly, and watch the "likes" pay him in sugar. Pleasure: bump the algorithm with a new documentary that looks virtuous enough to justify a late night. Flexible truth: let him describe this new habit to others as "a season of reflection," which means nothing and changes nothing. Friends: book his calendar with low-cost social warmth. Rationalize sin: help him call early bedtime "self-care" when it is, this week, cowardice away from a difficult but fruitful conversation.

Do you hear the tone of my counsel? It is not panic; it is hatred. I hate this because it is so little and so stubborn. For years, we taught him to love the grand gesture that burns out. Now the Enemy courts him with small fires that train the hands. A sentence. A sink shared. A pause. These are nails we cannot pull with spectacle.

There is one more matter, and I write it here because I do not know that I will have another chance to say it to you without an auditor reading over my shoulder. You must never look directly at Him. You must never let contempt for the humans harden into contempt for the One who takes their side.
You flirt with that posture in your jokes; you mouth something like bravery; it is not bravery. It is tin. The older among us do not say His name because we remember what happens to the mouth that says it without permission. We do not even spell it to ourselves. I do not warn you out of piety. I warn you out of survival. There is a sound that comes with the smallest honest prayer, and it is not music; it is a weight. We spend entire careers teaching men to dodge it. If you hear it while you work, do not pretend you do

not hear it. Withdraw. Work another angle. I have watched fools stare and stiffen, then crumble. Our Master does not shield such fools. He does not shield much of anything truth be told. His shield is a rumor. But I have no patience for martyrs of stupidity.

I expect you to report tomorrow not with a tally of his entertainments (boring), but with the two questions that now matter: Did he read? Did he tell the truth to someone with a pulse? If he did, I want names, timestamps, interruptions. If he did not, I want the names of the interruptions we employed so I can reward the clerks who filed them. There is nothing like a commendation to sharpen the claws of the petty.

And if – if – he persists if the thread becomes a rope and the rope pulls him toward the sort of confession that does not taste like theatrics, if the kitchen becomes a chapel and the chapel becomes a door, then we will do as we always do in such moments. We will crowd the exit with mirrors. Let him admire his resolve. Let him narrate his awakening. Let him congratulate himself for seeing through our tricks. The Enemy can dissolve pride; yes, yes, He can. But He often allows it to sit a while, and while it sits we can sour the bread.

Before I seal this, a trivial administrative note, which I am certain is not connected to anything above and should not cause your hands to shake as you read. A summons has been delivered to my desk (curious timing) regarding "several irregularities in reporting and a pattern of near-losses that border on unprofessional." You know how jealous certain supervisors are of anyone with independent methods. They prefer their disasters spectacular and their victories filed in triplicate. Mine are neither, and therefore suspect. I will attend the inquiry after dawn. That I mention dawn is, as you will appreciate, merely a coincidence.

I will not dramatize. We are not in the theatre; we are in procurement. If the inquiry goes poorly, you will be assigned to someone with less patience and more appetite for noise. He will teach you to kick doors that should be listened at.
I do not recommend it. If the inquiry goes well, I will send you a list of new cases and we shall resume our slow feasts.

Between now and the sound of the first kettle, do the following without theatre. Silt his sleep. Bend his pride toward performance. Turn his proposed honesty into a small speech he can admire later. Attend especially to the second morning; first mornings are crowded with brave illusions. The second is where men decide if this is romance or marriage. Help him choose romance. It fades. Marriage does not, and it is the Enemy's favorite word for everything He refuses to abandon.

You will notice, finally, that I have not once said we have lost him. We have not. We may yet not. The path from pause to Person is lined with a thousand small choices, and we have standing contracts with most of them. I am only admitting what you must learn if you are to live long: that our victories are never final and our losses are never clean. We work in the fog, not flames. We are accountants of drift.

Sne me, before night ends, the names of the shows you will suggest, the messages you will float, the harmless chores you will place like pebbles on a prayer. Send me also a copy of the psalm he will likely reach for (he prefers short ones when he is starting new things; calculate accordingly) and three possible sentences he could text his friend that sound true while not being the truth. I will choose the best and forward them to Scheduling. If you are clever, you will include a sentence so pious that no one would dare ask him what it means. The safest words are the ones that close the mouth that speaks them.
I have written too long. That is another of the Enemy's tricks – He makes us talk when we

should be silent. I shall practice our own craft now and stop. Remember what this is: not catastrophe; not coronation. A moment. All our scaffolding can lean back into place if we adjust the screws. It is just a lamp, after all, and he is not good at lamps. Perhaps the screw will strip again. Perhaps the child will not laugh tonight. Perhaps the friend will sleep through his alarm. Perhaps the psalm will look flat. Perhaps the sink will leak. We have many perhapses. He needs only one Name, and I will not write it.

Quaver

Yours in persistent subversion,

Quaver
Senior Associate Tempter
Infernal Department of Soul Acquisition
ffice 6B, Third Circle Annex, Central Pit C

Editors Postscript

The letters you have just read were not submitted voluntarily. They were recovered from an internal archive whose exact location will remain undisclosed. Suffice it to say, they were never meant to be opened by human hands.

I cannot confirm whether "Quaver" is the true name of the author or simply the title assigned to this particular operative. Internal records show nothing before his appointment to the Department of Soul Acquisition – no birthplace, no training history, not even the usual entry evaluations. He seems to have appeared in the roster already mid-ranked, already fluent in the Department's rhetoric, already dangerous.

The recipient, "Pipwick," has likewise vanished from the personnel logs. This is not unusual. Trainees either vanish quickly due to catastrophic incompetence or vanish later due to catastrophic promotion.

The case reference in these letters – one "Elliot" – remains unresolved. This is partly why the documents have been made available to the public: to serve as both warning and encouragement. The patterns described here are not antique.

They are not unique to one soul. They remain in circulation, retooled for every generation.

A final note: when these pages were first examined, the last letter bore faint scorch marks along the bottom edge. The archivist who handled it swears she heard a sound while reading – something like a laugh that wasn't coming from her throat. The document was quarantined for three weeks before being cleared for release.

You, read, may choose to treat these letters as satire, as allegory, or as something else entirely. But if at any point during your reading you recognized yourself in the descriptions, I would suggest you treat that recognition as more than coincidence. Some correspondence, it seems, is addressed far more personally than the envelope suggests.

– The Compiler

About the Compiler

The Compiler prefers to remain unnamed. Over the years, he has collected unusual fragments of correspondence from sources most people would consider either unreliable or impossible. He claims no special authority beyond an unusually persistent curiosity and an unwillingness to look away from uncomfortable truths.

His previous publications include *The Unsaid Minutes: Notes from Conversations That Never Happened* and *Directory of Places That don't Appear on Maps* – both of which sold modestly and raised more questions than they answered.

When asked why he risked publishing this particular set of documents, the Compiler offered only one sentence:

"Because some letters should be intercepted."